REFUGEE TALES

VOLUME III

Edited by
David Herd & Anna Pincus

First published in Great Britain in 2019 by Comma Press.
www.commapress.co.uk

ISBN 1912697114
ISBN-13 978-1-91269-711-3

Proceeds from this book go to the following two charities:
Gatwick Detainees Welfare Group and Kent Refugee Help.

The publisher gratefully acknowledges the support of Arts Council England.

Supported using public funding by

**ARTS COUNCIL
ENGLAND**

Printed and bound in England by Clays Ltd, Elcograf S.p.A

Contents

Prologue

THIS SONG IS TO ANYBODY
Whether alone
Or in community
Those keeping
Or in observance
Those who
Shall be held

It is from the trees
Who listen out
To those as well
In association
From the ground
As the season falters
In recognition everywhere
As call to change

Anybody
Who seeks
Against perhaps the backdrop
Of the mountains
Set forth solely
For the purpose
Susceptible
To any act

Who would be held
As once they had
Whether political
Or jurisdictional
At the time even
When it was committed
At its dissolution
Turned back.

To anybody who stands
Or who had imagined
Standing
Watching the roof smoke
Against the perimeter
Witnessing the constitution
Fall

Who knows
At dead of night
That this is actually
The circumstance
Within the burden
Of each state
Who is denied
The law

Who would act
Or would be held
Anybody shall be subjected
In the quiet
Before it was applicable

Who stood listening to the birds
Or pictured that they might
Imagining
A full equality
As they carried that acoustic
Waiting as the language
Turned

To anybody
Who sleeps
Whether alone
Or with belongings
Who occupies
The background
As the earth
Curves

Who stands
This dead of night
Whether left
Or in association
At that time
When it is committed
Who would walk
Towards

The Stateless Person's Tale

as told to

Abdulrazak Gurnah

You ask how long I have been here. This is now my twelfth year, and sometimes I have to count more than once to be sure I have the right number. It is so long. I have been coming and going between the Home Office and one office after another in all that time. When I say Home Office, I don't mean I go there or meet anyone, I just receive letters. Do this, do that, otherwise. They don't like it if you don't cooperate, let alone if you dare to disobey. Everyone knows that behind the letters there is a list of threats, withdrawal of privileges, detention, deportation.

That is what they are waiting to do, to deport me. They have been wanting to do that for the last nine years, ever since my arrest in 2009. I was sentenced to over a year in prison which meant I was liable for automatic deportation upon release. The courts do that deliberately, give sentences of just over a year to make it possible for the Home Office to deport us if they can. The reason they do not always succeed is because there are laws and there are lawyers with good hearts who stop them, or at least delay them. Also they cannot deport me unless the country they intend to send me to is safe for me and is willing to accept me. As you know, my country is G___ and I fled from there because my life was in danger, but the Home Office say that it's not so dangerous any more, and I can return safely. I don't think so. Whatever they say, G___ will not accept me because I have no papers to prove that I am from G___.

I have applied to be recognised as a stateless person. If I was stateless, then I would have residence, I could work and contribute to the country, and after a length of time even apply for citizenship. But even that is confused. Although the law required me to apply to be recognised as stateless, the Home Office keep sending me back to the embassy for travel documents so they can deport me. I have been to the embassy three times now and each time they turn me away because I have no documents that prove my nationality. The woman there laughed at me this last time. 'You're still here,' she said. 'The Home Office are wasting your time sending you to us. How many times have you come to us? The answer will always be the same until you come with papers to show you are from G___.'

I have no choice but to go to the embassy when the Home Office ask me to, otherwise they will say I am not cooperating, and they will put me in detention. I am liable for detention at any time, that is my status. I don't want to complain. They tell me to go, I go.

Why do I not have papers? I am laughing at my ignorance and because of my bad luck.

When I was in G___, and in hiding from those people who wanted to kill me because of my Christian work against cutting women, there was an English man who helped me, Bernard. He worked for the Christian NGO which employed me. He knew that my life was in danger because the people who were looking for me came to the office several times to ask for me. I was desperate to get away, and it was my English friend Bernard who advised me to come here. He took my passport from me and a week later he gave it back with a visa stamped in it. I asked him how he did that as usually it is very difficult to get a visa: you have to attend an interview, pay a lot of money and send the passport to another country for authorisation and it all takes a long time. He said don't ask, so I didn't. Somehow friends and relatives helped me raise the fare, and my English friend Bernard and I travelled together to London.

I was so grateful to him for everything he had done for me, and for also accompanying me. I had not travelled to Europe before and it was reassuring to have him sitting beside me. The airport officials asked me some questions and I answered as well as I could without really understanding why they were asking those questions. I must have given the right answers because they let me in as a visitor. When we were through the gate and in that crowd of arrivers in the terminal, my English friend Bernard asked for my passport. He said it was safer for him to keep it and that I was to go to the Home Office and say I have come for asylum. I gave him my passport and he gave me a piece of paper with the address: Home Office, Lunar House, 1st Floor, 40 Wellesley Road, Croydon CR9 2BY. In a moment he was gone, and I have not seen him since.

I don't know why I gave my passport away so easily. I trusted him because he had helped me so much already. I don't know why he took my passport. Perhaps it was out of good intentions, to help me. Or perhaps it was to protect himself, because I don't know how he obtained the visa for me, but it was probably not done in the proper way. Perhaps it was to protect whoever had helped him. It was soon after he disappeared into the crowd that I realised that I did not know how to find him again. I realised that I did not have any money, and that it was a weekend day and the Home Office in Croydon would not open until Monday morning. Even then, I had no idea of the long journey I was about to embark upon.

As the office was closed, a security guard gave me the address of a place I could stay overnight. Then the following day I went back to Croydon where I was questioned and interviewed and sent to temporary accommodation. It took me several weeks to understand that the officials did not like me, that they intended to get rid of me if they could, that perhaps they did not believe my life was in danger in G___. They turned down my application to stay and the refugee advisers told me to appeal. I was turned down again and appealed again. It took months between application and rejection and appeal. By this time, I was living in Glasgow and was becoming slowly defeated by my idleness. I had to stay at the address I was allocated. I had no money, just a card for my basic necessities. I could not travel and worst of all, I could not work to earn a little extra for myself and to keep my mind and body healthy.

Yes, it was looking for work that led to my arrest. I went to register for work using false documents. I used false documents because I have no documents to prove my nationality. The papers belonged to someone who was in the same congregation as me in Glasgow. He had permission to stay and could take a job, but urgent family affairs meant he had to go back home. His family were going to lose their land if he was not there to contest. If he went back to his home country, he would lose his refugee status and would not be able to return, but he had no choice. I borrowed his papers and went to register for work at an Agency. I don't know how the agency worker knew that the documents were not mine. He did not give any sign or challenge me. He asked me questions about myself and what work experience I had and what work I was looking for. Then he said he had to go and fetch a form or something like that and would be right back.

The police turned up within minutes, two cars with four men who were happy in their work. They took me away and locked me up, and the next morning I was in court. They were in such a hurry to get everything over with that they did not allow me to call anyone or speak to a lawyer. I was not charged with attempting to register myself for work as someone else, but for being illegally in employment. I don't know why. Maybe it made their case stronger. There was no evidence, no discussion, no defence. It was all over within minutes and I was sentenced to fourteen months in prison, and liable for deportation on release. I was sent to prison; no, I don't want to talk about that. I was given early release after a few months, and was sent to the Dungavel Detention Centre in Strathaven. It is where they hold people waiting to be deported. From Dungavel, I was sent to another Immigration Removal Centre and after several months there I was sent to S___ where I still live now, back to the round of application, rejection, appeal. I have been living in that house so long now that I feel in charge of the others who come and go. I make sure everyone does their share of cleaning and clearing up. No one makes a fuss. There are two men from Eritrea, just boys really, a man from Ivory Coast and a Russian. Yes, a white man... Russian, not a Chechen or a Tartar or one of those other kinds of Russians. Sometimes I think he must wonder what he has done to be put among an African rabble like us.

When the police arrested me and the court sentenced me in such haste, there was no time for me to collect any of my belongings or my documents. I asked about my papers and I was told there was nothing there. Everything was cleared out after my arrest, the photograph of my wife and children, my school certificate, my birth certificate, my address book. They must have thrown them all in the bin. So when the Home Office advised me to go to the embassy to get travel papers so they could deport me, and even paid my fare to London, I had no papers of any kind to prove I was from G___. As you know, this did not stop them from sending me again, and again. Perhaps they did not think I was trying hard enough, or perhaps there is no thinking behind it, just a machine which is programmed to be cruel.

I have been here now for twelve years as I told you. I am still not allowed to work. I help at my church and volunteer for an organisation that visits and counsels hostel dwellers. Many of them are alcoholics or ex-offenders. I was given eighteen weeks training for this work, so I am a qualified counsellor. I registered for an Access course, but I couldn't get a student loan because of my status. I also did an Adult Social Care course which a refugee organisation paid for. I do what I can to try and stay sane, but it is hard when I have so much time on my hands and so many sad memories of my children who are so far away and have grown up now. I am 59 years old and I feel the time going away from me. I have constant headaches, high blood pressure and just recently I was diagnosed with diabetes. The doctor said I am depressed and prescribed me medication for it. I said I don't need medication for depression or stress, I want my freedom. Many days I don't even go out.

I know that my only chance now is to be reclassified as a Stateless Person, to have an opportunity to start again, but I have been waiting for years for a decision on that. My last application was a year ago, as a result of which I was sent once again to the embassy where I was told what I was told before. No papers, no G___ travel papers. I don't want to go to G___. My life will be in danger there. I need to be reclassified as a Stateless person so I can have the right to work and contribute something to this country.

Why is the Home Office so wicked? Is this what the English people want them to be like? They can't all be wicked like this. Many of them have been so good. Perhaps after all this time someone in the Home Office will say let us end this poor African man's torment and let him work. What have I done that they are treating me like this? If they turn me down this time, I'll pack my bag and go to the Home Office and tell them to send me where they want, even if it is only to dump me in the middle of the ocean.

The Orphan's Tale

as told to

David Constantine

YES, SAID M. We liked the white people. I know all about Poppy Day. My grandad served in the British army. He was proud to be a man from Freetown, fighting for the nation that had abolished slavery and now must defeat an evil that would enslave the world. Never forget your origins, he said to M You're descended from slaves the British set free and gave them a beautiful country to call their own. And when the civil war stopped and there was a Poppy Day again, he put on his uniform and his medals and marched with his few old comrades to the cenotaph in George Street. M ran alongside, very proud of him. I had no mother and father by then, he said.

M has told his story many times, in all sorts of situations, to a variety of listeners. Every storyteller wants to be believed. Belief persuades. Every storyteller wants to be persuasive. How willing to be persuaded the children are who sit on the floor, children from the world's four quarters who sit crossed-legged on the magic reading carpet in spring, in the sunlit classroom, the walls of it lively with their artwork, and a T.A., from Kashmir perhaps, or Somalia or Iraq, reads them a story and sees how their eyes widen in amazed belief. Such a trove of stories they have in them already, those Year-Twos.

M wants to be believed, to persuade, to get them to feel the living truth of it and be moved to pity. At first he thought the plain facts would do the trick, but when he paused in relating them he looked into faces which were dubious. He was easy to catch out. This now doesn't match that then. He was new to the game and they were old hands and to be honest (they said) sick to death of it. One case was much like the next in their experience. The harder M strove to be persuasive, the worse he became at it. Knowingly or not, they had stirred an old terror in him. He was young but his terror was primeval and now it had woken in him he muddled things up – dates, names, locations, past and present intentions. Pretty soon they hardly needed to ask him anything. He slipped from trying to remember and answer in good conscience to trying to guess what they wanted him to say. Pretty soon he was all at sea and in a sudden rage he said things that would be taken down – almost sorrowfully, as it seemed – and used in evidence against him. We have made enquiries, they said. You had a grandfather. Why did you leave him? The war was over, things were looking up. Could you not have worked hard where you were and repaid him his love and kindness in his final years? He told me I must go, said M Seize your opportunity, child. I did as I was told. Ah, they said.

M should perhaps have stuck to the fairy tale which his questioners did not exactly disbelieve, only they couldn't quite see how it should tilt the balance in his favour. He should have become his own barrister and stood, so to speak, aside from himself and said, Shall all this child's good fortune, all the kindness of strangers, all his determination to be worthy of it, shall it all count for nothing now, go to waste, all be in vain? I ask you. But he was not very eloquent. He pointed to the facts. Surely they spoke for themselves? Surely they outweighed the letter of the Law? They shrugged. Not necessarily, they said. Pretty soon, after their treatment, when he floundered and got flustered and lost his temper and began to tremble because the horrors – the girl, and the two boys with machetes, for example – were rising up in him and choking him, causing him to weep and sweat and shake in present terror, in that state, of course, what Mother Country would think him a good investment?

Mother and father dead and on the streets countless children, old as pain, sick with witness, speechless, many lacking hands to pray or beg, he was chosen by a reputable charity as one who might recover and even prosper in a rich and Christian country famous for its love of justice. He was out on his own kicking a football hard against a wall when the charity man fetched him in. M stood looking at his grandfather, who said, Go with my blessing, child. I shan't be around much longer. He had no ID, no papers whatsoever. Never mind, said the charity man. We'll see to that. And so they did. At Lungi International and Heathrow he was spoken for. Exit and entry without let or hindrance.

And the English Borough! Used to processing people like M, again they did their best, which in his particular case was so good you might have shown it to the Angel as a thing in our favour amidst so much weighing heavily against us. Having got him registered, they steadied him and with good sense and kindness helped him on his way; and first into the care of a Mr and Mrs Robinson who had two small children of their own. Never in telling his story did M forget that beginning. I was an orphan, he said, and you gave me a house and home. I was hungry and ye gave me meat: I was thirsty and ye gave me drink: I was a stranger, and ye took me in. I had the clothes I stood up in and you dressed me fit to be seen wherever I went.

The school, named after a pleasant local river, was used to children arriving out of the blue. The lingua franca was a vigorous local English. It served a catchment area rich in mother tongues. In M's case, and not just in his, the home of the tongue was thousands of miles away and the mother herself did not speak it nor any other language now.

M was eager to learn. He saw the point. It would steady him in this new situation, it would give him a footing, if he listened to his teachers and studied hard. At the first Parents' Evening they smiled on him and on Mr and Mrs Robinson. If he continues like this, they said, he will do very well.

It should also have counted in M's favour that he was obedient. Or say he was anxious not to offend. Stay clear of the Law, said Kev, his social worker, quite early on in their relationship. The Law in that understanding, as it pertained to M and people like him, far from being a fatherly friend you could turn to for protection and advice, more resembled the adversary, the devil, who walketh about seeking whom he may devour. Best keep out of its way. Kev, who had seen a thing or two, after a couple of years watching over M, at their final meeting smiled and said, Remember: keep your head down. This was not *quite* the same as, Stay clear of the Law. He saw M happy, looking about him with a very open face, and in a more primitive age he might have said, You don't want them noticing you – 'them' being the gods, some of whom might be riled by the sight of a mortal having too much of happiness. M took Kev's advice to heart. It accorded with his own feelings. But he was a child, becoming a young man, and happiness is very seductive; so of course there were times when he dropped his guard. Playing football for the school, baby-sitting the Robinsons' twins, riding his bike round the park and along the river… And once – it was after finishing GCSE's and before the results came out – it was in an ice-cream parlour, they had commandeered three tables in the window, half the class were there, loud and silly, with only a pane of glass between them and the general public passing on the pavement in the sun. Was this an occasion when some jealous deity, perhaps alerted by a spy on the street, looked down and singled M out and muttered, Enough's enough? Questioned, looking back on that sunny afternoon, asked to answer for it, M would have had to admit, You are right. I was happy. I was heedless.

And if that – laughing in public – was, as Kev might have said, asking for it, how much more so was what came later: Céline and her five-year-old daughter, Lara. That was hubris, a monstrous overweening.

Briefly, then. In the holidays, after Sixth Form College, encouraged and helped by Kev (who got him a National

Insurance Number), M worked six days a week in a supermarket, stacking shelves, or, nights, for more money, in the warehouse, unloading the deliveries. He opened a bank account, he gave Mr and Mrs Robinson something towards his keep, he had cash and a card of his own for a social life, he paid tax. His self-esteem went up a notch or two: *I am useful, I contribute.* And he met Céline. She was with her daughter and she asked him a question to which – she admitted later – she already knew the answer. His quickness and good manners made her smile. He led her to the Rice Krispies. Thank you, she said. He bowed. Then into a silence the little girl asked, What's *your* name? M, he replied. My name is Lara, she said. M crouched down and shook hands. Very nice to meet you, he said. Thereafter in the warehouse he wished he were in the aisles.

Céline was three years older than M and both at this new outset had reasons to be wary. They saw each other now and then, not by arrangement but not quite by accident either. Once in the supermarket Lara wandered away to the end of the aisle and out of sight into the next. When Céline missed her she was reappearing and said, That man you like is round there. M was near to finishing his shift, so they waited for him outside. Then went to the ice-cream parlour and sat in the window, the three of them. Soon after that she invited him round. She had a council flat near the railway station. She told him her story and he, hesitantly, told her his. He spoke almost in a whisper, she had to lean close, her child was at the kitchen table, drawing, and seemed absorbed. When he halted, shrugged, and said that was enough for now, they looked at one another with different eyes. Anyway, you're safe here, she said. Yes, he said. I don't think about the bad things, not often at least and not for long. And he told her about his foster parents and how he looked after the twins for an hour or so now and then. She was silent, contemplating him. Lara likes you, she said. Perhaps you would look after her if I asked you for a little while now and then. I have to go to the school sometimes and the Council and the DSS and the doctor's and the C.A.B. and all that, and I can't

, Mum. Hearing this, nodding his head, M
, he felt the tide of good fortune had set his
.ising and lifting him and he would be borne
. He was exultant, and at the same time abashed.
.at she asked felt like a gift he was called to accept, and
.ke a temptation that for his own good and hers he must
at all cost resist. And soon there was more between them. He
accepted and gave and what he gave she likewise accepted as
though it would be hurtful, insulting and a sinful folly to refuse
what each was offering to the other.

I'm eighteen today, said M. And he was thinking, I like lying
in the dark. Why didn't you tell me? said Céline. Did you tell
anybody? Mr and Mrs Robinson knew, he answered. They
asked me when I went to live with them and I told them the
day my real mother and father and my grandfather said it was.
But I haven't got a birth certificate so who knows when it
really is? She told me this morning her grandmother got here
in the *Kindertransport*, on the very last train. Me being eighteen,
I suppose. You can do all sorts of things when you're eighteen,
said Céline. But nothing better than this, he whispered to
himself in the dark, invisible. Say again, said Céline. Nothing
better than this. I thought that's what you said. I love you for
saying that. Still, if I'd known I'd have baked you a cake and
bought you a present. I looked after Lara, he said. Hardly
anyone gets a present like that. And now this, lying in the dark,
rain against the window, the talk going between them so very
soft and close. I've been thinking, he said, now I'm eighteen
perhaps they'd let me pick her up from school some days. If
we went to see them together, you could say who I am and
that I'm all right to look after her and help you out a bit. I've
got more time now. Also it looks like I'll be getting a council
flat. Somebody put in a word for me.

    M had more time because he was finished with the College
except for his results. All being well, he would go to university
next and study engineering, a three-year course plus one

(between the second and the third) in industry, after which, as everybody said, he'd not have any trouble finding a well-paid job. So, carefully arranging his shifts at the supermarket, he stood most days till the end of that term at 3.30pm in the school's front yard in a throng of parents, grandparents, guardians and other responsible adults waiting for the doors to open and the children to appear. He did not look odd, unless perhaps for his youthfulness, in that mix of people who had a common purpose there and who, however intently nattering with one or more regulars on the scene, all glanced continually at the closed doors or, like M, never took their eyes off them. On only his third day collecting he was addressed by a much older man with a yellowish pallor showing through his dark skin who said that after five years in this country and everything going well still he was fearful, still he had no faith, because – and suddenly there were tears in his eyes – where he came from, which was a very bad part of Iraq, he had seen more than one school bombed and children buried alive and the lucky ones, if you can call them that, dug out so burned and broken their own mothers hardly knew them. Hospitals too. Bad, he said, very bad. And in this good country where my wife and my children are safe and good people help us, why can I still not look at a school without hearing screaming and seeing blood starting through the dust and ashes on children's faces? And he raised his left hand open against the sky in a gesture that M did not entirely understand.

Some days, always without warning, Céline would suddenly be there next to him and take his arm. Then he did not know where to look in his happiness and pride.

The appearance of the children, this daily repeated ordinary thing, was a wonder to M. Two teachers opened the doors, stepped out and stood aside. Then came the children, the press of them through the narrows and their opening out towards the ragged arc of the grown-ups waiting. Their noise, a babbling, a loud susurration, was that of the lingua franca and if this was their mother tongue, they continued in it. But many, seeing kith and kin, broke into different speech, they tuned themselves to home, they passed without halt from one belonging, in one set of sounds, into another. M observed this, he took it in, got it by heart, and would never let it go. This was daily, this was normal, this was the custom, the working arrangement. He saw that the children did not emerge warily into the open air but came out to find what belonged to be there, love in place, there waiting, trustworthy, out of the safe school they came into the expected welcome. The babble in the yard was like wild-life sounds, the generations mixed, the throng was augmented, mothers with prams and slings embraced the elder siblings and gratefully accepted the day's offerings of paintings, writings and colourful fabrications. Then the school doors closed, the crowd of mixed humans went out through the iron gates and very slowly, with lingering partings, conversations to finish, broke up into various lives throughout the town. Some days M and Céline walked home with Lara between them holding their hands and relating the day impartially in equal measure left and right. But most days he had sole charge, he carried her bag, held her hand tight, conducted her through the people, across roads, listening, asking a question now and then, but mostly listening and all the while attending, watching out for her in her blithe carelessness, right and left and right again, with an adult's proper caution, bringing her safe home.

M got the keys to his council flat. Céline and his foster parents helped him move in. Then, with their encouragement, he applied for a new job, better paid and more interesting than the supermarket, with a long-established firm who dispatched belongings to people moving abroad. Nothing ruled out, they said. Tell us where and by when – and relax: we'll see to it! Belongings of all shapes and sizes, to wherever you wished. The idea of helping people move house where they liked, across oceans, continents, the hemispheres, appealed to him. You'd be an accessory to freedom! Something to be proud of. He named one teacher at school and two at the College as his referees.

Within a fortnight he heard they had taken up references; a week later he was invited for interview in ten days time; the day before the interview they wrote to say they had done the necessary checks and had found that he did not have the right to work; next day came a letter from the Home Office informing him that since he was now eighteen his discretionary leave to remain in the United Kingdom had been revoked. He must apply for indefinite leave to remain and pending the outcome of that application he was not permitted to work but must report weekly and sign in at the Office in the Borough. Mrs Robinson phoned the lawyer. M had a nice note from the supermarket. They were very sorry to have to let him go. So it began.

Tremor through terra firma, cracks through the walls and ceiling of the living room. And a clean white hand approaches and between thumb and finger takes hold of the end of a thread and delicately pulls. The unravelling has begun. Some pathogen has been insinuated into the web of his life. It eats the little love-knots and the subtle connections. It is a sovereign undoer of living intricacies. Its handler knows where he lives, knocks at his door, informs him that henceforth the sitting tenant – love – must cohabit with fear.

Idle cruelty? They halt his progress, re-christen him Illegal, order him to show himself at their counter every Monday morning and with a signature record that he has not absconded. And then – they are very busy, there is a backlog, forever increasing, of people like him – they let him be. True, he can't work; true, he can't study to become that very useful citizen, an engineer; but he may walk the streets in the likeness of a free man; nobody says he must break with Céline – on the contrary: take the child to school every morning, collect her every afternoon, if you wish; do the shopping, learn to cook, what's stopping you? Not us.

Where he reports they are friendliness itself. Nasrin, Olly, Piotr, they greet him cordially, he signs in a trice, they smile, he is gone. He is the obedient kind, compliant, very anxious to placate, not to be annoying, not to give the Law reason to do its worst to him. In that office, the decent men and women behind the desk are accustomed to faces like his, eyes like his, suppliant, wishing only not to offend. They know that he feels himself to be at the mercy of the Law. He will do as he's told. He hopes it will earn him reprieve.

Week after week he presents himself. Cycles there, signs in, cycles back to Céline's, and does what he does every working day: tidies up, goes shopping with her list and her money, cycles to his own flat to check for post, and soon it is time to fetch Lara. He is useful, Céline gets a few more hours. They eat together, two or three nights a week he stays. The routine begins to persuade them. They are not really so very unusual. She works, he does much of the house-keeping, they burden nobody. But all the while they know they are increasing the life under threat. Against the facts – which is to say, against the Law – the life in each of them clamours for more and more. Now they are not cautious. Their waking souls watch one another in wonder and delight. All lovers have a creation myth, how the world was made anew, how they themselves began, a stock of stories, what their first deeds were, what they meant, what they mean now. They believe their fictions, could not live without them, lying side by side they recount them, with variations, new possibilities. And one thing I want you to know, said M and I tell it you now because I am frightened that I won't own it later on, if very bad things happen. Kev told me to keep my head down, and I think he meant I shouldn't let them see how happy I am. Too happy, they will come for you and stop it. But I swear to you, Céline, I will never believe we were foolish, let alone that this here and now is a crime. It is against their Law, I'm sure of that, but it isn't wrong. I'm happier now than I belonged to be and I'm very proud of that. It's fit to show to the dead – and in my life there are a lot of dead – I show it and say to them, See, I have not forgotten you, you can take pride in me, you gave me a chance and I did not squander it. You don't think we are fools and criminals, do you? For answer, mouth to mouth, their tongues necking in silence, M and Céline, breathe more of the demands of love into one another's lungs. They desire to be one flesh, to become indissoluble. M falls asleep first, as though the defiance has exhausted him. She lies a while longer, thinking. Sleeps then; and always and every night now, as a mother hears her waking baby, she hears the first whimper of his nightmares, she lies next to a young man in the toils of the horrors he witnessed in a lawless land. She smells the rank terror of elsewhere, older, far older, than either of them, deeper, vastly extensive, the darkness under the earth that those who have been wounded in their souls will helplessly open to and live again if into the sanctuary comes the least reminder of the evil. Gently she slaps him awake, she quietens him, in the aftershocks of terror he weeps with shame. And this – her single combat for her lover's life and soul – only furthers their ingrowing into one another. Increase the love, increase the loss: the equation is ungainsayable. Nonetheless they must fight. They are in a mortal struggle against the Law. Reporting weekly, he is the very image of obedience; but together under one roof they are in revolt, they will not play safe, they will not stint one another in love. They will raise the banner of what they have to lose. They will say to the Law: see what you are undoing.

Every Monday he is afraid. He has seen men and women taken as they sign. Nobody hangs around. Having signed, they get out fast, reprieved for another week. But in the queue they whisper in the lingua franca the latest stories, some fantastic, all credible. Ali absconded, he daren't go home, he rides the Circle Line, he kips in a bin, which is safer than the cemetery or the bus shelter, he attends the food bank, looking nobody in the eye. Friend of mine, says Maliki, her lawyer swore she was safe and sound, then they came for her at five in the morning and drove her into Scotland and imprisoned her there. Different jurisdiction, see. She has to start again. Distance is a great disheartener among the powerless and the poor. How shall a woman take the kids to visit their father if he is in a hostel for the homeless three hundred miles away? Or from behind the wire how shall he bid her be brave with no credit on his phone and the reception lousy at the best of times? Sever the connections, tear the web, a human quite alone is an easy thing to manage. And visiting time – it might be your last – a man in a uniform bawls, No touching! Weep if you must, but only across the table.

One Monday an older man, Algerian, asks M how long since he had the letter. Five months, he answers. Maybe they've forgotten him, maybe they've lost his file. It happens. Him over there – a Palestinian perhaps, older by his look than the Algerian – it's been three years. I had a friend, Liberian, they let him alone nearly seven. Then he saw them waiting when he pushed open the door. He ran. No sight nor sound of him since.

M doesn't tell Céline what the Algerian said. Two weeks later, as he signs, he sees in Nasrin's eyes that they have come. He turns, they nod, they handcuff him. They wear the uniforms of a private enforcement company. He makes no protest, says not a word, but begins to shake. He is a young black man in handcuffs like any common criminal in a public place. Later he remembers an absolute silence and dozens of faces turned his way in fear and pity.

They take him into a waiting room and empty the contents of his shoulder bag and his pockets on to a table. Wordlessly they sort through these few small belongings, take his phone. Only then do they uncuff him and with a nod convey that he's at liberty to put everything back. He tries to speak but the words will not come out. He tries again, they observe him coldly. He manages to say, as if through a speech impediment, I have to phone my partner to tell her she has to collect Lara if I can't. You're collecting nobody, one says. We do the collecting, says the other, and hands him his phone. Be quick. He phones, no answer, he leaves a message. I've been arrested, I can't collect Lara. One takes the phone and puts it in M's bag which the other slings then into the corner. You get that back later. M asks can he not go and fetch some things from his flat. My bike is just outside, he says, as if to be helpful. They don't bother to answer. You sit quiet, one says. Sit over there and don't move. You're on CCTV. He pours him some water into a thin plastic cup. They leave the room. Two other guards come in and sit by the door, saying nothing, watching things on their phones. Every so often somebody else is brought in handcuffed. Same procedure, same degree of courtesy. All the enforcers sound East-European. M sits for five hours, during which time they bring in nineteen men and women. A soft babble of languages. An Arab boy leans his elbows on the soiled table, covers his face with his hands and weeps. The tears well through his fingers. An elderly black woman goes and sits by him, puts her right arm round his thin shoulders. There, there, child, she says. One of the guards, coming close, orders her to desist. She looks up into his face, a look of such withering contempt, he shrugs and goes back to playing with his phone. M takes note, as though the encounter might one day fortify him. Then the guards consult a list. One nods. The men and women they have rounded up are allowed to retrieve their belongings from the heap in the corner. Then they are escorted through the main office, where there is still a queue, to a waiting bus. November, already dark. The bus pulls away through crowded streets, people shopping, going for a drink, going home. In the bus the captives in several languages, in tones of great distress, begin to phone. M has a message from Céline. Not to worry, she has fetched Lara. He phones and tells her he could not do the shopping and he has her purse with the house-keeping money in, which he is very sorry about. No, he doesn't know where they are taking him. Tell Mrs Robinson, ask her to please tell the lawyer.

That night, in a privately run Incarceration Facility, sleepless with two other men in a cell that stinks of its toilet, M for the first time hears what he will often hear again in the years to come: the howling of captive fellow human beings who have

23

been told that early next morning they will be on a plane back where they came from, however bad that place and whatever their loves and friendships, their loyalties, brave beginnings, notable achievements and aspirations here in this worsening land.

The Foster Child's Tale

as told by

A

I HAVE BEEN STUDYING social work at university for two years now.
I like it.
I like the stories.
And social work – I guess people in general – well, they're all about the stories.
Everyone is full of pages, every part of our bodies is a different chapter.
We are all just walking novels.

My problem is that I am still trying to understand my own story.
Some of the key pages are missing.
Some of the key characters are missing.
I don't really know the beginning, let alone the end…

★

I don't know what country I was born in.
I don't know what my date of birth is.
I don't know who my biological parents are… or were.

My earliest memories are from when I was around four years old. I understand that my foster father had rescued my foster mother and her son from India, where she had been sold as a prostitute.

A

I think I heard somewhere that my foster mother couldn't have any more children so they took me in.
From where, or from whom, or from what... I don't know.
Who knows.

I was around five when my foster mother died of cancer.
My foster father used to drink a lot, and after my foster mother died sometimes he was hospitalised.

We stayed in a garage for a while in the capital city, until we got kicked out of there and I was sent to live with an aunt, my foster mother's older sister.

★

I was ill-treated there.
I was given the job of carrying grass from the field back to the house to feed the animals.
I had to clean up the cow shit and look after the chickens.

When I complained, I was beaten.
One phrase sticks in my mind: 'You were found on the streets, you are not our blood, do as you are told.'

One day, when I was out collecting water, I met a guy who told me I could escape back to the capital if I walked for about an hour away from the village, and got a bus.

I remember sitting on the roof of the bus because I had no money for a ticket.
I remember bumps on the road and the cold wind down my neck.
I remember ducking out of the way of swinging trees.
I must have been about six years old.

★

I tried to find my father when I returned to the city but he had left the area we lived in.
I had nothing and I grew hungry.
I saw other kids on the street begging and I joined them.
I remember being told that if I sniffed dendrite in a bag then my stomach would settle.

I remember older kids stealing the money I had been given.
I remember the men who would come at night.
I remember the police beating us.
I remember waking up one morning after sleeping rough in a temple and one of the other boys had died in the night.
I remember, I remember…
When maybe some things should be forgotten.

★

When I was about nine, I was introduced to a man named Serge.
He was the founder of an NGO set up to assist street children like me.
He is perhaps the first hero in my story.
There would be others, but he was maybe the first.

He clothed and fed me.
I started to feel safe.
I went to school and excelled.

But when I tried to do the equivalent of A-levels, I was told I needed a citizenship card.
I needed evidence of my story.
But to get a citizenship card you need a birth certificate, and I had nothing.
I was introduced to a man who was involved in political activities.
A citizenship card appeared and soon after Serge sponsored me to come to the UK as a student.

A

★

I remember arriving in London for the first time.
The darkness and rain could not dampen my excitement or my
sense of hope.
Elephant and Castle felt a long way from home...

Things took a dramatic turn in 2014 when I was told that
Serge had committed suicide.
My sponsorship stopped and I was unable to pay my fees for
the second year.
I returned home to ask the charity if they could help me, but
they declined as I was over eighteen years old by this point.

It was during this time, that a huge earthquake struck my
country, killing thousands of people, including some of my
friends and their families.
A Biblical chapter.
Trauma, shouting, flashbacks.

★

I returned to the UK only to experience another, second,
personal earthquake: immigration detention.
My university had reported my situation to the Home Office.
From the reporting centre, I was bundled into a van.

The windows were black.
There were three other people in the van.
More stories.

I didn't really know anything about detention before they took
me there.
My friend told me they only detain people for 24 hours and
then you are released.

As soon as I entered the detention centre and I saw the faces, I realised some people *must* have been there more than a day.

I asked my roommate how long he had been inside.
I still expected him to say a few hours.
When he said he had been there for eight months, that's when I felt all hope leave my body.

★

I was terrified in detention.
I didn't know what was going to happen to me.
I had no idea what was going on, and no one gave me any information.

I was detained for five days before they moved me to The Verne, in Dorset, far away from anyone that could visit me.
They took me at night.
I was scared.

I remember asking the guard, 'Why me?'
He said, 'The people who are flying soon are kept in detention centres near to the airports.'
OK then, I thought, 'So, I'm not going to be removed any time soon… But then why am I being detained?'

I felt like I was being put into some kind of human storage facility.
Altogether, I was in detention for two and a half months and they transferred me *four* times.
Each time I was moved *just* before I had an appointment at the legal surgery.

★

I felt cheated.
I started to get more and more anxious.

A

I couldn't sleep.
I felt like I was in custody for no crime.
I felt caged.

I found all the shouting, the screaming, very difficult.
More flashbacks – the earthquake went off in my head.
The aftershocks still ripple today.

★

I was released at the end of March 2016.
I am still getting used to life outside detention but it is also clear that detention goes 'beyond the walls'.

Whenever I see guards in uniform all the bad memories of detention come back to me.
Or whenever I eat noodles – the same kind they gave us in detention – I think about The Verne.
Detention is the chapter that keeps on going.
No full-stops.

★

After I was detained, I wrote a letter to my pre-detention self.
I needed to find out if he still existed.
Sometimes I think he might be coming back.
Other times I think it won't happen.

★

Dear Pre–Detention Self,

It's been such a long time! I haven't seen you for almost a year! I feel like I don't know you anymore! Where the hell have you been hiding?! Why didn't you get in touch? I thought there was no secret between you and me. Is everything still good with you? Are you still hopeful and moving forwards towards your goals.

I remember the last time I saw you was at Alex's birthday, at the Queen's Head. You were so talkative, making fun of everything. You wouldn't let the conversation drop for a second. Are you still like that? Do you still want to be a computer engineer? I remember you were in the middle of your studies the last time we were together. I remember your friends asking you whether you were ever going to grow up – you seemed so happy to be in the present moment! I remember you smiling a lot… and enjoying the odd lager (or two!) as well. Are you still playing football with your friends every Monday? Are you still wearing those Nikes you loved?

I have to admit, I had to collect ALL my strength to write this letter. I am writing it in difficult circumstances. It's not quite how it used to be for me. Laughing in the pub feels a long, long way away. I wish we could go back there, and be together again – you and me.

I've just come out of detention. I was detained for about three months. It's too much for me to explain everything about what happened to me there in this letter. But it is an experience you would never want to even dream of. I hope you never go through something like that.

Do you remember when you and Ram and I got locked inside Ram's flat that time? Well, imagine that but for three months. Only without each other to talk to. And without the food we wanted to eat. And without sunlight coming in. And without the sofa or the bed. And without the peace of mind of knowing the door would open at some point and we'd go outside. Imagine that we were also surrounded by other people who look like they're experiencing the end of the world – some people are screaming, some people are silent with fear, some people are crying. Some people try to kill themselves in front of you. Imagine one night a stranger in uniform comes in and drags Ram out the door. And you don't know where he's gone or if he's ok. And the lock on the door turns again. And it's shutdown.

Well, this has been something like my reality over the last few months.

When I came out of detention I had nowhere to go. I was nearly homeless. I had no one to talk to. I had no one to go to the pub with. No money to buy anything. I had no one to play football with. I really missed you then. It would have been good just to see you around. Even just to sit together and have a small chat. Even just to sit together in silence.

I think detention changed me a lot to be honest. I wonder if you'd even recognise me now if we saw each other. You'd probably think I was someone else. I wish we could get back together and hang out. I wish we could get back the old vibe we had, back then.

I miss you. Do you think I'll ever see you again?

Wishing you all the best my friend,

My Post-Detention Self

The Son's Tale

as told to

Monica Ali

WHEN I WAS SEVEN years old my dad died and everything changed. He was a chartered accountant, the first in his family to go to university. He was a good man. His family were proud of him, he achieved so much… but they never accepted my mother. I don't know why.

She had three children from a previous marriage, and my father provided for them as well. He treated all of us as his own. Perhaps his family couldn't deal with the fact my mum had been married before. Even to this day it bothers me that I don't know why they hated her. But they did, and it affected my life in a big way. They said terrible things about her, called her a prostitute.

I remember two things about my dad. He wore brown leather shoes with a square toe. 'Pointed shoes,' he said, 'always look cheap.' Every week he lined up his shoes, four pairs each with a different pattern of holes to decorate the toecaps, and we polished them together. Hard brush for the soles, medium to sweep the dust from the leather uppers, then the polish goes on with a cloth. A soft brush to work the polish deep and a clean rag to add shine. For me it was never a chore, it was a ritual that I loved. The second thing I remember is my dad's laugh. It was sudden and colourful, like a firework display. When you heard it, when you witnessed it, his whole body exploding, it made you clap your hands. He was so full of joy.

It exhausted him though. Afterwards he always wheezed and coughed.

When my dad died, his mother – my grandmother – took me to live in a big family compound on the other side of Lagos. She loved me but she was old and too weak to take care of me herself. I was passed around to aunties and uncles. One of my uncles was the reverend of a big church next to the compound. The church had stained glass in the windows, blue, pink, orange, green, scarlet. White hibiscuses grew outside, a row of sunflowers, and there was this plant with deep green leaves and lovely little red flowers that guarded the lawn. If you tried to go across, your legs got torn to shreds. This plant is called 'crown of thorns'.

So there was beauty, but there was also ugliness. Many people came and went, some for prayer and sermons, others for something else. For two years I didn't go to school. My education stopped. I was passed around. Sometimes I had no food. More often I was beaten. And I was abused. Not just by one person. Many people. I never told anyone until I married and told my wife.

For three years I didn't see my mum. She was struggling, with my three half-siblings to raise, and she wasn't welcome at the compound. Then one Sunday she appeared at the church like a vision. It felt like a miracle. I thought I was dreaming, but then she put her arms around me and she smelled sweet like roses, like she always did, and I knew she was real. From then on, I was allowed to visit her at the weekends. I was happy for the first time since my dad passed away.

One day I got injured playing football, a bad cut on my leg. I hid it because my uncle had forbidden me to play football. If he found out he would be angry. He had a thick red electric cable and he used to beat me with it. I didn't dare show my wound. It became infected and I got tetanus. I couldn't walk properly. Somehow I made my way to my mum's house and she took me to the hospital. The doctor said I was lucky. Another day later and they'd have cut off my leg.

My mum was furious with my uncle about my untreated injury. She took me back to live with her. I was twelve years old. I was happy to leave that compound where they beat me and abused me. But I never told my mum about any of that. It's common in Nigeria. And if you are sexually abused the shame is on you. It's not something you can speak about.

My mum had a boyfriend, a policeman. He beat me and he beat my mum. This too is common in Nigeria. I'd try to get him off her, but I wasn't big enough. We didn't have phones to call the police. You'd have to drive to a police station, and anyway the boyfriend was a policeman himself. The day he left we finally had a peaceful house.

Not a whole house, because we were poor. We rented a couple of rooms. My mum's hands were always raw from her work, and from washing – clothes, the floors, dishes, children, even my football. She was a big believer in washing. 'God wants the world to be clean,' she said. 'He didn't make it so you could mess it up with your dirt.' She worked in a palm oil factory, but she didn't have formal employment, it was all a bit around the back, and sometimes she had no work. I worried about her because she was so thin. I told her to eat more but she laughed and said she was dieting. I knew she was lying but I didn't understand why. I couldn't finish school because you had to pay so I worked in a factory too. And my mum was sick a lot of the time. She didn't tell me she had HIV. I was so angry when I finally found out, because I used to go with her to the hospital and wait outside and she never told me the truth.

Two weeks after she died, I came to London. I've been here for eighteen years now, since I was a very young man. I came here illegally. I came here because I wanted a better life. This is how it happened.

In Lagos I had a friend who was born in the UK. He lived in Lagos but every year he went to London for a holiday. I was very close to him; we were like brothers. Whenever he went away, he came back with a present for me. When my mum passed away, this friend heard about it and asked if I wanted to go to England. He had moved to London by then. I wanted to go but I didn't have money. My friend said he would give me a loan and I could get a job and pay him back later. I said yes. There was nothing left for me in Lagos.

I used his Nigerian passport which had 'Right of Abode' stamped in it. He had two passports, this Nigerian one and a British one. I didn't have any passport of my own; I'd never even been on a plane, had only seen them on television. I did everything wrong at the airport. Stood in the wrong lines, went the wrong way, was so nervous I was sweating… but I was lucky. The lady just let me through.

I moved in with my friend and found work easily. My first job was serving at a fast food kiosk at a station. Then I worked in a shop selling sports goods. Afterwards I did night shifts in a factory, packing and loading trucks. I've always been a hard worker. I like to work. It makes me feel good to do well at a job. When I got offered a job with a security firm, I was proud. Even my friend couldn't get a job like that. When I went for an interview, he said I wouldn't be accepted. Everyone told me that. But they took me. I was sent to work as a security guard in a department store. They have stores all over the country and I worked in one of them, in central London. After a while the manager of that store wanted me as the head of security. So I resigned from the agency and I was employed directly by this prestigious company. I was working hard and I felt I could make something of myself, but of course there was a huge problem. Many problems.

I couldn't have my own bank account. Because I was using my friend's identity, everything I earned went into his account. I had borrowed around £3000 from him. After four years he was still taking everything from me and giving me a few pounds here and there. Also, he changed. When I lived with him in London, he began ordering me around. I had to report to him. In the middle of the night he'd wake me up and tell me off, shout at me about small things – I shouldn't eat stew twice in one day, I wasn't allowed to do this and that. I'm not a pushy person. I'm not confident and I try to please so I put up with a lot. Anyway, I was stuck. I didn't know how to move, what to do.

I was dating a girl, and eventually she convinced me to leave my friend. She helped me find a room to rent. When I moved out my friend wouldn't let me use his identity any more. I managed to get a National Insurance number and keep working but I got scared when the Inland Revenue started investigating and I left the job.

I couldn't pay rent after that and went to stay with a friend in a big, shared house. That's when I got involved in criminal things.

What I did was wrong and I don't blame anyone else for it, only myself. I am the one to blame. When I was staying in this house there were lots of us boys – young men – coming and going, all involved in crime. I learned from the others how to commit fraud. I used cards to buy stuff in shops and online. I applied for credit cards using false identities and used them knowing the bills would go unpaid. I bought clothes, electronics, phones, all sorts of things. I sold them to a guy at the phone shop and he sold them on again. He was my friend.

This is how I was living and my girlfriend wasn't happy. Her family wasn't happy. She always prayed for me. A couple of times she got pregnant, but she was still studying at university and went for abortions. I didn't agree with her doing the abortions. There were a lot of tensions. When she had just started a master's degree, she became pregnant a third time. When she had another abortion, it broke us up. That was the destruction of me. I blame myself. I didn't have patience and I had lost the only good thing in my life.

I moved out of the big house and lived on my own in a studio flat. One night I met a girl in a bar. She was pretty and I liked her. I gave the girl and her friends a lift in my car to some party they were going to. The next day I had a call from an unknown number and it was her. She said she dropped an earring in my car. There was no earring in my car. She just wanted to see me again.

We fell in love. Like that, very quickly. We wanted to marry so I went to ask her parents and they wrote a list for the dowry. This is how it is in Nigeria, it's the tradition, and though the girl was born in this country, her parents keep to these traditional things. I was glad to bring what they asked for – money, brandy, fruits, vegetables.

We married in a church. It was done properly. I got my own passport, a real one, from Nigeria House. We needed that to make the marriage legal. The wedding was the same date in May that I came to this country, the same date my father died.

The next year we had our first baby, a girl. And at the end of that year I went to the shops to buy a present for my wife's birthday, using a fraudulent credit card. I was arrested. They discovered my immigration status and after two days in a police cell I was sent to a detention centre. Reality kicks in from there.

On my second day in detention an official came and gave me a plane ticket. A lawyer helped me and the ticket was cancelled. The police were investigating me and they found other cards after my arrest. I was released on bail after three weeks and when my case came before the court, I was sentenced to 26 months. I served thirteen months, first at a maximum-security prison, then at a prison for foreign nationals.

In prison I signed up to lots of courses – information technology, business studies, all sorts of things. I never had the opportunity before so I took it. I was the gym orderly. I was the offender representative on committees. Maybe it sounds strange but when I was in prison, I had the chance to do things that made me feel proud. On the outside, I was ashamed of the things I did.

I was eventually released from prison. I was on bail from the immigration court and had to sign on every week. For three years it went on like that. I couldn't work legally and I was afraid to work cash in hand so I was at home looking after the children. We had three children by then. My wife was working, and we managed. I loved being with my kids, two girls and a boy, and I was glad to look after them.

When the deportation order came I appealed against it, but the appeal was refused. I was in absolute fear. How could I live without my children? How would I live in Nigeria? I have nothing in Lagos. I have nobody there.

The marriage was falling apart. I wanted to make it work but I didn't know what to do, and my wife started drinking. She started using drugs. I was desperate. I heard that in Ireland it's easier to get Irish citizenship with a European family stamp. That means if you have a wife and kids who are British you can get an Irish identity card. We moved to Ireland for that reason. My wife was reluctant but I persuaded her.

I got the Irish identity card and it gave me a bit of hope. I loved Ireland, I loved the countryside, but my wife hated it there. She kept going to London. She even went there for Valentine's Day. When she came back, her wedding ring was gone. She said she'd sold it. I knew she was having an affair. She was still drinking and doing drugs, and I looked after the children. As soon as they came into this world, they became my life.

My wife moved back to London, taking the kids. So I came back too and stayed with a friend. The marriage was over and my wife had another man. I picked up our children every day after school and I took care of them every other weekend. It worked okay for a while but then one evening I had a call from my daughter who told me she was at home on her own. She was only seven. I must have sounded shocked because then my daughter told me not to worry, that mum left her alone at home all the time. Of course, I spoke to my wife about it and this is how she responded: 'If you have a problem, why don't you report it?'

She knew, with the deportation order hanging over me, that I was powerless to do anything. I'd be put in a detention centre or on a plane. From Nigeria I wouldn't be able to help my kids at all.

It went from bad to worse. The family support worker at school tried to help. We agreed days for me to pick up from school and times for me to drop off at her house. I didn't have anywhere for them to stay with me, just one small room. So I'd keep them until around eight in the evening and then drop them off. Many times she wasn't there. One time, when I had to have them overnight because their mother had disappeared again, the mother of one of the men who lived in the house gave my children £10 each. So I bought them some clothes, clean pants for the next day, stuff like that. I only had £4. I'm not allowed to work and I can't get benefits. I survive somehow, with the help of friends. That woman was so kind. She didn't have much and she didn't have to help us. Sometimes you feel everybody just fights for what they can get, but there are good people in this world.

Soon after, the boiling point came. My wife texted me to say she wasn't going to be home that night at the time when I was supposed to drop them off. These are little kids, they need to go to bed so they can get up right and feel right at school. So I took them to mine and put them to sleep in my bed, and because I did that, she came round – it was late in the evening – and kicked off. She was screaming and hitting me and then she called the police and told them I had snatched the kids from her. When the police arrived, she told them I had a deportation order. I was arrested, taken to the police station, and then to the detention centre.

I don't even know what to say about that place. I don't know where to start. It's worse than prison. It's a place filled only with despair.

On the second or third day, I went to see a welfare person, someone who is supposed to advise and help. The first thing she said to me was, 'Why don't you take your children and go back to Nigeria?'

I cried a lot. I found it hard to eat and became very thin. I couldn't sleep. When I did sleep, I had vivid dreams. I never dreamed like that in my life before. All the time I dreamed about my two girls and my little boy; they were always in danger and I couldn't protect them. And I dreamed about my mum. In the dreams she never liked me. I was falling apart.

But I understood something about my mum, at last. I used to blame her a lot because she didn't tell me things, because she gave me away when I was only seven years old… I always loved her but in one piece of my heart I blamed her as well. I see it differently now because I realised that all she was doing was trying to protect me. That was the reason she kept secrets, the reason why she gave me away, the reason she took me back again. She didn't hate me. I used to think that, but now I know it's not true. As a parent you get to understand.

For three months I didn't see my children. Their mother never brought them to see me. She told them I'd been deported.

I had a hearing in front of an immigration judge. You can't get legal aid so I asked a friend who asked a friend, and a lawyer – not even an immigration lawyer – agreed to help me. On the day of the hearing he didn't show up, so I stood up in court and represented myself. I was glad because I wanted to speak. I wanted the judge to hear me. I wanted to tell her who I was and how I came to be in that courtroom in front of her.

The judge had hard lines on her face. She frowned the whole time. And she kept asking the Home Office people, why has he been in detention for three months? She seemed cross about it. They couldn't give her a reason so she told them to release me. They had to let me go.

Now I am trying again to get my deportation order revoked. I fill in endless forms and make phone calls, but I don't hear anything from them. I understand why some people – perhaps many, perhaps even most – would say I should be sent back to

Nigeria. I came here illegally. I committed crimes.

When I came here I was very young and all I could see, when I travelled on that false passport, was a lifeline. I got thrown a lifeline and I caught it because I wanted to survive. It's not an excuse but it is the truth.

I don't blame anyone but myself for the things I did that were wrong. I was involved in criminal activity, and served time in prison. But I believe everyone deserves a second chance. I've never had a chance to show my real identity, to prove who I really am.

I'm not a bad person. I want to do good, not only for my children, for this country as well. I love this country. This country changed me a lot. I've been here nearly eighteen years now. I want to work. I want to be known as a good person. I want to be a good man, like my dad.

Most of all, I'm scared for my children. They need me. I'm their father and I'm like their mother too. They want to live with me. I never enjoyed my childhood and I don't want my children to go through any of the things I had to go through. I fear for them.

The Father's Tale

as told to

Roma Tearne

At 1 pm, the time of the birth, the father is unaware of his son's momentous entry into this world of air, and earth, and water. The sun has burnt away the thick mist lying on the ground and spread late warmth on this mellow September day. The father's bed, there is an airport nearby, vibrates gently. But with no window in the cell he cannot see the passing planes. Life for him is a door being locked and then unlocked from the outside. Steel chains mark out the endless days. For him.

I am an animal with a human brain, he thinks, dully.

Still, even he must admit the nine months in captivity have gone quicker than expected.

'Time to have your lunch,' the warden says, casual but not unkind.

And no, there has been no news. Not yet.

'First babies take their time,' the warden says, a slight softness creeping into his voice at the thought of his own child's birth. 'You'll hear soon enough. Perhaps when your visitor comes.'

'It's a boy,' the visitor tells him, arriving a little breathless with the glad tidings. 'Yes, yes, you have a son. All's well, mother and baby are doing fine!'

The new father shakes his head, tears and smiles arriving simultaneously, taking him by surprise.

'A son?' he asks, incredulous, now. '*My* son?'

'Yes, *your* son! Congratulations!'

At that the visitor reaches out to embrace the young man, who, with these simple words catapults into fatherhood.

'No touching,' the warden calls, sharp-eyed and expressionless from behind his desk. 'You know the drill.'

They do; no human contact of any sort. New father he may be, but rules mean rules.

Correct?

Correct.

Besides the father is due for deportation at any moment. With no warning he could be sent back to the place where *he* was born; a place of lurking danger, a place where life most likely means a torture chamber. Once out of sight the warden knows, this father like all those in this place, will slip out of mind. So why waste emotional energy on an embrace? Still, this brand-new father has other things on his mind. For now he cannot think beyond two simple words.

Kure min?

Words spoken in his mother tongue from 30 odd years before. Spoken by that distant, loving voice. Remembered now in this cataclysmic moment.

'*Kure min.* My son!' he says again, eyes shining, pride arriving all unannounced. Love in a time of displacement catching him unawares with its astonishing primeval power.

'Yes, yes he's yours. Forever,' the visitor tells him, speaking lightly, hiding his private misgivings.

For how can this older man forget what lies ahead; the stumbling blocks, the heartache? Still, first things first, the visitor tells himself firmly, holding out a folded sheet of paper to this new father.

'Take it!'

The visitor has smuggled in a photocopied image. Some kindness does exist, then?

'Look! See! Your baby son!'

The new father looks and, astonished, sees how the

newborn boy rests in his mother's arms. *His* son, he thinks again.

At that his brave new world with all its rich layered aspirations shifts imperceptibly, rendering the new father speechless. For was not an earthquake occurring in this godforsaken place? Something lifts the corners of his heart and everything he once believed in changes in an instance. The sun, the moon, other people's children, this detention centre, the wardens, life itself, is different. Love needing no further help from him begins to grow in single-minded abundance.

'We have to get you out,' the visitor murmurs before leaving. 'Until Thursday, then,' he adds, raising a hand in farewell, never touching, leaving this brand new father staring at the pale photocopy; all that he has of the child he should now be holding in his arms. A stateless baby born to stateless parents.

'We'll have to think of a name,' the father says, beaming, waving goodbye before going obediently to be locked into his windowless cell for the night.

Outside the evening's drawing in. And although the September sun has lost its bite, summer still lingers in small traces as the visitor turns his car around and leaves the detention centre. Barrier raised and lowered to let him out. A coiled barbed wire fence scribbles pencil lines across the rosy sky. A plane hurries along the runway and is airborne, destination unknown. While somewhere on a ward on British soil, new life lies gently sleeping. Five hours old, all unknowing.

Once, long ago, the child's father had been born into a fragrant land of light and heat and dust. Loved by his large family, he had been strangely clear-sighted from a young age of his country's flaws. For boys like him in the ethnic minority are unwanted. The majority, he soon sees control everything. He understands too the dislike that people have for any kind of difference. And although he cannot as yet comprehend, at eight he sees his people being persecuted.

At twelve he runs away from school, disturbed by the violence he has witnessed.

At eighteen he refuses to join the army; his biggest crime to date.

'Why join an army that kills our people?' he asks his father. 'It could be you, or my uncle or my brother that they make me kill!'

His father's face remains in shadow. How can he advise his idealistic son?

'So go,' his father says at last, never guessing how long the journey will be. How hard the road, how far his son will have to travel, how many lorries he will cling on to, what different kinds of sorrow lies ahead.

'Go, then. With my blessing.'

And so the young man goes, travelling on a road fraught with peril. He is caught again and again, beaten, tortured, screamed at by men who look just like him.

Six times in detention, eight more in prison.

Ah! But England, *England*, the agent promises, is very different.

'Worth paying money to reach, worth hiding in a lorry, worth risking life and limb, huh?'

Time comes and goes with different locations and events. Prison, detention centres, papers, regulations. For thirteen years he lives this way, in transit. A bird without wings on a wire that has been broken. Forms filled, lost, and filled again. Time bends into infinity with money sent from home by broken-hearted parents to corrupt, well-fed, complacent lawyers. By now the not-yet-a-father is being systematically broken. Young guards, old guards, faceless managers, pitiless rules, all designed to punish and torment him. Cruelty is the currency he lives by. The world he has by chance been caught up in is a frightening place. Those who linger here will end up insane. The 'hostile environment' promised by the British government has been created precisely with this end in mind. Designed by humans to break the human spirit. These days the rich and powerful bottle inhumanity and sell it to the displaced. And underneath this poisoned air, rage and helplessness thrive in equal parts.

But then, as sometimes happens, Fate steps in and alters the course of events. And on a spring night in a brief spell when he is released on bail, the young man meets a girl. It is a night of moonlight and intermittent showers. At home, he remembers, the almond trees will be in bloom. His mother will be resting in the yard, his father smoking on a seat nearby. He thinks of his parents knowing that they are growing old without him, missing him in the awfulness of this enforced separation. The girl he's met is young, alone like him, and youthfulness makes them laugh together in spite of everything. And when finally he manages to ring home, his mother's voice too sounds young again, alive with happiness for *his* good fortune. Soon, she tells him, after their wedding, there must be a grandchild for her.

'By blossom time next year,' his mother says, laughing.

'Yes,' he promises.

'Yes,' his future wife agrees shyly when he tells her.

Having granted him this brief respite, Fate again intervenes, and not long after the marriage ceremony his appeal for asylum is refused. Once again he is back in detention. Once more his father sends money for legal fees. More money for more useless lawyers, will this cycle never end?

'Please,' the young man tells the judge, speaking by video link from his dark place of detention, 'I must stay. I am newly married, my wife is pregnant, now. Please. Let me stay.'

The administrator turns her stony face to the wall. The lawyer disappears. The judge he speaks to is replaced by another.

'If you send me home, they will imprison and torture me. Please, I must stay.'

'Sign here,' the administrator says.

'We have issued you a ticket,' the administrator tells him. 'You will be leaving just as soon as all the paperwork is done.'

'I will be tortured if I go back,' the young man cries again. 'Don't you see?'

They don't. The global connection exists only in name. What happens elsewhere does not matter here. Die if you must, but do not come here with your tales of human abuse.

After the announcement of his possible departure, the father-to-be has a visit.

'Hold on, hold on,' his visitor promises. 'I'm getting you another lawyer. Believe me when I say, this one is decent and will not touch your money.'

But the new father can hold on no longer. Dying surely must be easier? Bit by bit his mind is failing. Some things cannot be recovered, he thinks in panic.

Tying a sheet around his neck, would that do the trick?

When they find him they stuff him full of pills. Stupid man, you're off your bloody head! In hospital he thinks about his weeping wife and feels shame. He is a man who wanted only simple things; to live, to love, to work, to have a home. Is this too much to ask? The baby, his child, is kicking in the womb.

'Therefore,' the faithful visitor tells him, firmly, 'you *will* survive.'

Now, in these first hours of his new son's life, night moves slowly. Somewhere out of sight, a moon is shining on the world. Owls glide noiselessly through the trees, sheep huddle peacefully in pens and foxes roam across the green and pleasant fields. Tonight the sea is quiet, as if it too is holding on as all across its darkened towns and cities, the good people of this blessed isle sleep on. Even the warden at the centre drops his guard, nodding slyly off. What harm can come with the detainees locked up for the night?

In this way the lights go out like the tide and all, save for our new father, sleeps.

My son, he thinks. My son! Already the words are familiar. How has this happened so quickly?

In the bunk above him, the father's roommate has cried himself to exhausted sleep, leaving the night to our new father alone.

'Wait my son,' he murmurs, rocking gently on his bed. 'I will be with you very soon.'

But, at dawn they wake him up abruptly.

'Hurry. You are leaving for the airport in two hours.'.

'No,' he shouts, backed against the wall, frightened. 'My new lawyer says the paperwork allowing me to appeal will be with you at nine o clock, I have a chance to stay.'

'Sorry, mate. You leave today.'

There are fourteen of them waiting with handcuffs, for one single man. Too many to get into this tiny room, but each very willing to hold him down if necessary. A doctor will accompany him on the flight.

The new father is screaming now. Have you no pity?

'I have to make a phone call,' he shouts. 'I want my solicitor, my friend, my wife.'

But time, it seems, is of the essence and soon they have the father belted and handcuffed ready for departure. Hastily, they bundle him into the van.

Outside the world still sleeps, indifferent to his plight. The owls glide home after the night, the foxes return to their den to feed their young. Early travellers, arriving at the airport, yawn tiredly, their tattooed feet flip-flopping, their sun hats tied to rucksacks stuffed with airport 'reads' ready for the beach.

Is there time for a cup of tea before the flight?

In a maternity ward in some distant hospital, all is quiet. The stateless baby sleeps at his mother's breast. He is just fourteen hours old. Occasionally he startles, arms stretched out in the way new babies do. And then he clutches at his mother, while she, still tired from the long and protracted labour, rests fitfully. Who knows what she dreams of? There is no one here to see her lovely face, no flowers stand in water beside her bed, no welcome-to-this-world cards or presents.

As dawn breaks, they stir. The baby begins to feed, eyes tightly closed, jaw working, tiny hands splayed across his mother's face. Bliss in human milk. While unknown to them the child's father speeds through this season of autumn mists towards the secret heart of the busy airport. A place no holidaymaker will ever see.

'Please,' the new father says, once more, 'please. My permission to appeal will be faxed to you at nine. Please wait.'

He speaks in whispers now, all hope gone, the happiness of yesterday a distant memory. Perhaps, he thinks, his mind bludgeoned with this terrible grief, they will let me speak to her? But where *is* she? What hospital, what ward? Five men sit with him in the van. Two others stand outside for a smoke. The administrator and the doctor take all the paper work and disappear into the airport just as another plane speeds across the runway. The sky above is beginning to lighten slowly as time passes.

Back in the maternity ward, the cleaners awaken the new mother. Staring at her son's face she sees his father.

'He will be coming soon,' she promises. 'Any day now.'

This young girl is all alone and frightened. She needs her husband.

Two planes thunder past, then another and another.

'Well you are very lucky,' the administrator says, angrily tossing papers. 'What a waste of time, they've cancelled your flight. Let's go.'

'I told you I would be granted permission to appeal. Can you take my handcuffs off?'

'No!'

'My hands are hurting.'

'Shut up.'

Back at the detention centre, once again the new father is shaking uncontrollably. His legs give way and the men, his minders, force him up before locking him in his room.

'I want a doctor!' he shouts, but steel doors cannot answer.

'I need a coffee,' sighs the administrator, blank-faced and exhausted, glad she has only one hour left of her shift. When she goes home she will take a shower.

But when his visitor arrives the new father cannot cease weeping, for with relief comes a second, harsher outpouring of grief. The easing of tension comes at a terrible price. Can grief kill, wonders the visitor, appalled by this poor man's plight? Yes, release has been granted. Yes, he *can* visit his son now.

'What's his problem?' asks the day shift's warden, puzzled. 'He's going home isn't he?'

Home, thinks the new father and all at once he sees that 'Home' is a word needing new definition. Home is now being pared down to the barest essentials. New life waiting on this alien soil has made it so. A filthy room, a family who at last can sleep together, skin brushing skin, that missing sense of touch, *this* now means Home. Here, in this unforgiving island, he's found his home. All, then, is not entirely lost.

But even so, still three months of inefficiency has to pass before, at long last, the new father's eyes can drink in the sight of his child.

Still now this father is a wiser man, remaining cautious in his newfound happiness. This time, he thinks, he will not forget. The journey isn't over yet, more asylum applications lie ahead, not one but three. Before the next great battle of their lives can be laid to rest.

The Volunteer's Tale

as told by

R

Home

My name is R. I grew up in a small village in Sudan, in a small family. I had just one brother. My sisters got married and moved away with their husbands when I was still little. So growing up, it was just my dad, my mum, my little brother and me.

My family were farmers. My dad farmed, while my mum helped at home. When I was little, I just wanted to help my dad because he worked by himself, and so until I grew up, that was what I tried to do. I have to say my life was ok while I was little. Working with my father with the animals – we had camels, cows, and sheep – I was happy because I only had relations with my family. I didn't know anything about the wider situation.

I don't remember how old I was, exactly, when I started to get to understand the situation. Where I'm from it's not easy to know your birthday, so nobody knows their age precisely. I have to just guess. I remember I didn't ask my mum how old I was before I left.

But when I got to, maybe, fifteen years of age, I began to see that the situation was changing, especially for the young people, the boys. I kept trying to help my family, because, as I said, my mum and dad didn't have anyone else to help them. And I tried to keep helping them until I got to, like, seventeen years of age. By that point, I was starting to know about the wars that were happening around the place. A lot of people were killed – we had a very bad government, and the government had different militias, like the Janjawid who used to come to our village. Sometimes they tried to take your possessions, things like animals or whatever, by force. I remember, one day my dad was going to the market. He had some stuff he wanted to sell there along with everyone else. A group found them, you know, in the street – he told me this, I didn't see it – they stopped them, searched them, and took what little money they had, as well as most of their produce. They didn't go to the market; when they came back they had nothing in their hands.

From that time on, our lives changed completely. When you went to sleep at night, you didn't know if you'd wake up in the morning. Sometimes they would arrive suddenly and take people, kill people, things like that. One day I remember I wasn't on the farm, and this group came to my village and took all the men my age. They arrested them. I was lucky that time, because I wasn't at home, I was away working with my dad in another town. When I came back, I heard everything that had happened. I was terrified, you know, that maybe one day they would come back and arrest me.

It was another day like that one, when they arrived. I was sitting with my group of friends in the centre of the village, chatting away, when suddenly, like, five or six cars appeared. They began circling the village, everyone could see them. And then people just started being killed. My friends and I just started to run but there was no way to get out because they had circled the village and were shooting. That was the day I got arrested.

Until they arrested me, I never thought the day would come when I would leave my family. I was the only one helping them and they were getting old, you know. I had to look after them. When they arrested me, that was all I could think about: who would look after them? Was I going to live or die? Was this it? They put something over my eyes, and they tied my hands behind my back. That was the last time I saw my village or my people. That was the last time, when they covered my eyes.

That was maybe six years ago, or maybe nine. It was the last time I saw my parents and my brother. Since that time I haven't seen any of them.

They took me to a prison. They called it a prison, but it was not like prisons you see here. It was just, like, a room without windows. But I have to say 'prison'. They took me there by force – all the time I couldn't see anything, I just listened to their voices not knowing where they were taking me. Until in the end I found myself in a small, dark room, just by myself. Then one morning, they came, like, three people. One of them led me to a chair, with one of them standing behind me and one of them sitting in front of me and they started asking me questions.

The first question they asked me: Are you a supporter of the other side? Because we have opposition groups, and some people work with them. I didn't have any relation with those groups, I told them. I only help my family. They didn't believe me. Instead they tortured me, day after day, and beat me with something – I don't know what it was. They said, 'That's not true.' They said to me, 'We know you work with that group, and you support them. Sometimes you take them water, or food, or things like that. And sometimes you pick up information and take it to those people. We know you do.' I said, 'I don't have anything to do with them.' But every day they came and asked me, because they thought that maybe I was going to change my account. But I told them, 'Even if you want to kill me, I'll say nothing. If you want the lies, they're the lies, but this is true.'

After fifteen days, I remember, one of them came and spoke with me. He said, 'You have to come and, you know, clean the toilet.' That was the first time I got to leave my room, and I met two other prisoners in the process, one of them a friend of mine who'd been arrested with me. They took us to their office. Because I was outside of my room, they didn't let me open my eyes. I had to keep them closed until I found myself in the office. After we were done they took us back to our rooms. The next day they took us to the office again, but this time I caught sight of two guards, one of them standing behind us, and one of them just sitting in the corner. After a few moments, waiting, my friend whispered that the second guy had left his position. Shortly after the guy standing behind us left as well. And we said, 'OK, we haven't got much time. This is our chance to escape.'

But the wall in the yard outside was too high. And we said, 'OK, so, what are we gonna do?' We knew we had to be successful if we tried; if they caught us at it, they'd just shoot us. And we said 'OK, better than staying here. We have to try. Maybe we'll be lucky. If not, we'll all just die.' So we ran at that wall. We helped each other. The first one we had to help push over the wall, with the second one we had to take off all our shirts and make a rope for him to hang onto, that the first guy pulled. It was dark – not the daytime – we jumped over the wall.

After a few minutes, two soldiers came back to the compound, and not being able to find us, just started shooting. We ran. We didn't know where we were going – we just ran. Ran, ran, ran. We kept running all night, until morning.

Eventually we found, like, a small village. We didn't know where this village was, but we found it. We met this old man and we explained what had happened to us. But the man said, 'Maybe they're gonna come and find you if you stay here.' He asked me, 'Where do you live?' So I told him about my village and my family and said, 'The only thing I need of you is to send a message to my family or my village.' I told him to say, 'I'm alive and I escaped.' He said ok, he didn't mind doing this, he knew our village was quite far away.

After that we went to another village, bigger than the first. We went there and spoke to someone else about our situation.

This man said, 'I can keep you in my house for one day, but then after that you need to think about what you're going to do.' So we stayed there one day, and after that, the man helped us. He gave us money and he found some cars to take us to the city.

So we went to the city. But I had no money, no work, and no idea where I could go, I didn't want to stay there for long. Maybe if someone found me, they'd arrest me again. The first thing on my mind was I had to leave Sudan. I had heard of people travelling to Libya. But Libya is not easy to get to because we've got the huge Sahara between Libya and Sudan. And you need money as well. So I stayed there for, like, four or five days. But I still couldn't work. I tried to find people to talk to about my situation. Some people I spoke to were very kind and shared some of their money.

So I paid a person who took people from that city to Libya, by car. There were, like, fourteen of us in total, so they put us in the back of a Landcruiser. The man put something over the top of us – a net – and tied it in place. I was so worried about this, it was so flimsy, but I knew it was better than to stay.

So we started to travel – day and night, day and night, just driving, endlessly. When we reached the Sahara, I saw how few trees there were, only sand. And the desert is just too hot, you know. They only give you a little water, so you have to drink from small cups. You mustn't drink or eat too much, because when the water and the food are finished, there's no more.

Libya
So after fourteen days, we crossed the border between Sudan and Libya. There are Sudanese people living in Libya, but instead they took us to Libyans, and the problem was, they spoke with a completely different accent – Arabic, but different. We couldn't understand them, and they couldn't understand us. So that's one problem you have between Libyan and Sudanese people. There are other problems. Sometimes they started to just beat people, the soldiers, I mean, with the back of their

guns. You didn't have to talk back, you didn't have to say anything. Then they rounded us all up and put us in a container – a long container – and locked the door. For some time, you couldn't sleep, and you couldn't sit down because they hosed in water. You just had to stand there. If you wanted to sit down you had to sit in the water. Like that. And every morning they came and said, 'If you have money, you can be released. If you don't, you'll remain here – until you get money. Alternatively, if you have someone here in Libya, give us his phone number, and he can pay for you. Or, if you have your family's phone number, you can call your family back in Sudan.' That's how they got their money. I was there maybe twenty days. A lot of people died, you know – just out of hunger, or they got sick. And others, they were shot, point blank, in the face.

After that, they took us from the container to another place. I stayed there, like, ten days. I had no one in Libya or Sudan, because no one had a phone back in Sudan. In my village there wasn't anything like that – phones, electricity, television – nothing. So I told them I didn't have any phone numbers for family, or anyone here in Libya. They said, 'OK, you have to stay here then, until you die. Nobody knows you're here?' I nodded. 'So who's gonna know then,' they said. 'You have to sit there, stay there.'

Then one day a man came, a Libyan guy. He said, 'I'm looking for someone to work with me on my farm.' And I said, 'I used to work with my dad, so I've got farming experience.' The man turned to me and said, 'OK, you're going to work for me but I've got one thing you can't ask me.' And I said, 'What?' He said, 'You can't ask me about the money.' And I said, 'All I want is to leave this place, I don't want money. I'm not gonna ask you for money.' And he said, 'OK, that's good.' So he took me from that place to his farm.

At the farm, he had, like, tents, and he said to me, 'This is your room. Now I'm going to show you my farm, and the things you have to do here.' He had sheep and he showed me where the grass was, and where I had to take the animals to feed. And I had to open the water sluices every day or every two days. And the Libyan just brings me, like, lentils for the soup and something like spaghetti. This is what I lived on.

I worked on the farm for, like, four months. Then one day when he came back – he used to go for a couple of days then come back – I said to him, 'I told you I wasn't going to ask about money, but, you know, I've got a problem: since I left my country, I don't know what's happened to my family. I used to support my family, so if you don't mind, could I, you know, find someone and send my family money.' The Libyan said, 'This is the first thing I told you before I got you released, yeah? And I still tell you, you have to not ask me about the money. If you want to work here that's fine, if you don't I'll take you back to that place.' So I said, 'OK, OK forget about the money.'

Then he left again. After, like a month, I remember another Libyan guy came to the farm by chance. He asked me about another farm. I said that I didn't know about that one, I only knew this place. And he asked me, 'How long have you been working here?' I said, 'This is maybe my fourth or fifth month. And I have a problem with the guy: I've worked here five months and he hasn't paid me a penny.' He was shocked and I asked him, 'If you don't mind just helping me – that's all I want of you.' And he said, 'It's not easy. If I help you, maybe later I'll be putting my own life in danger. But I'll do it.' And he just took me by car and dropped me at a city called Sabha. He said, 'I can drop you at a house I know – some Sudanese people live there.' And I said, 'Thank you, you've saved me.'

He took me there and indeed I found the Sudanese. I talked to them and they helped me. They got together some money, and found a kind of taxi driver willing to take me to Tripoli. They knew the taxi driver, and spoke to him. The driver said, 'OK, I can help him but there is a problem with this guy; he hasn't got anything, an ID card, a passport, anything like that. It's not easy for me to just drive past a checkpoint. If they find him there, I'll get in trouble as well.' I said to him, 'So what can I do?' He said, 'If you're happy, you can lie in the boot.' I said, 'I don't mind.' So he helped me into the boot and I just stayed there, till we got to Tripoli.

And, you know, he dropped me there with another group of Sudanese people. I stayed there a few days, but Tripoli is crowded, with a lot of traffic and I'm from the countryside, I'm a villager. So I said to them, 'I'm not going to stay here because everything is crowded and busy. I'm going to find another city to live in.' So I left Tripoli and went to a small town called Surman and I stayed there for maybe a year.

But the problem is life is harder in Libya than in Sudan. In Libya, you can't walk, like, one mile from where you are and still feel safe. Everyone has guns, and if you walk on the street, someone will always stop their car, because they know you are not Libyan. They get out of their car and search you: if you've got money, if you've got a nice phone, whatever, they take it. This is the problem when you walk. And the other problem: even when you're at home, they sometimes come, like, four or five people, and knock on the door. Everybody has guns; they search your rooms, and take anything. Nobody can ask questions. Nobody knows if you're gonna be alive or dead by the end of it. Every day is like that.

And I just started thinking: *What kind of life is this?* It wouldn't have been easy to go back to my country, and it wouldn't have been easy to stay here. So everyday I just thought: *What am I gonna do?* I thought about my family and myself, and each day it got harder. So I heard about the people crossing to Europe. Even though it was difficult, it was better than, you know, staying there. And I got the idea that I should leave Libya. So I saved a little bit of money from my job, and I went to the city where people go from Libya to Italy. There I found a guy, who said, 'OK, you have to pay two thousand dinar.' 'I haven't got that kind of money,' I explained to him. I had lived there for maybe two years and I had saved, like, four or five hundred, something like that. And he said, 'OK, no problem.' So I gave it to him. After four days they took us to this other place, which was a huge place, and at night, maybe

900 people gathered there. 900, including children, women, old people, young people, families. They were all trying to flee to Europe. This was near the sea, of course.

Crossing

And I was shocked. All these people were going to cross the sea. We were divided in two, like 450 each.

That day, the first group left. The next day they took us, the second, to the coast where a boat – like a fishing boat – was moored far from the shore. You had to wade through the water. Sometimes the water came up to your chest, depending on how tall or short you were. Can you imagine, 450 people walking out to one boat? Seriously. In the end, when the captain came, he wasn't a Libyan. I don't know where he was from, but he wasn't Libyan When he saw us all in it, he said, 'I'm not gonna sail that. It's too heavy.' And they struck him with the backs of their guns. And he said, 'Alright.' He started the engines and he spoke with us. He said, 'So, if you're lucky, you get a new life. If not, that means, you know, these are the last moments of your life. Because it's too heavy.' And I thought, 'So, this is the last station in my life, so…' I didn't believe I was gonna make it. I'd been through a lot, you know, but this one, it felt like it was the end. And I just gave up. I said, 'Alright, if I die, you know, that's fine. So these are the last moments of my life.'

But we were lucky, and we got a second life. We got out of Libyan waters and across. And one thing I have to say: if it wasn't for the people rescuing us from the water, 100%, nobody would make it to Europe. So the Italian people – or maybe they were from elsewhere, I don't know where they were from – they came to get us. Water had started to come into the boat, because it was so overloaded. We saw a big lifeboat in the distance, but it wouldn't come close to us because it was too dangerous. So, you know, everybody started jumping in the water. I remember I was wearing my life jacket – but it was fake. In just ten minutes, the water had nearly filled it. I just jumped in because everybody was. They wanted to come and get us, but it wasn't easy. Then everyone else jumped in behind me. I started to swim, but I had a problem – the salt in the water started to mix with petrol from the boat and it became like fire, when it touched your skin. It was hot, and then it became too heavy to swim through. I know how to swim, but I had a lot of things clinging to me so it was heavy going. I just tried to, you know, get the things clinging to me out of the way. I went on like this for maybe 24, 25 minutes, you know. It doesn't sound that long I know. After that, somebody came by with nets. You had to hold them until you got to their boat. That was the last thing I remember. After that, I remember nothing, until I found myself in a hospital.

I don't know what happened after that. I found myself lying in this room; I could hear something, near me. It felt like a dream. I didn't know where I was or what I was doing there. I didn't know any European languages. I only knew Arabic. After a few minutes, the doctor came in. He asked me something but I didn't know what he was saying or what he wanted me to say. They brought an interpreter and they said, 'You are in Italy now, and you are safe.' After that, I started to remember the night before, when I had been in the water, and I remembered the others. So I asked them, 'What happened to the other people?' They said, 'We don't know. Some people are fine, some people are not.' After that I felt OK, I guess, although I had nothing and my skin was still burning.

After that, when I felt a bit better, I didn't talk to anyone; I just decided when the doctors had gone I would leave the hospital without telling anyone. And I just walked. I walked and walked. I walked to get to, like, a train station. And I found other people like me. We started talking about what happened, so I said to them, 'I came, like, I don't know exactly which day, but a couple of days ago, and I came from the hospital.' And they said they had lived in Italy for two years.

They said they'd all had their fingerprints taken, and asked if they'd taken mine. I said I didn't know how someone would have taken them. One guy said he had lived here maybe two years; then he went to France until they brought him back to Italy because they said, 'You have fingerprints in Italy'. He asked me, 'Did they take your fingerprint?' 'No, they didn't,' I said. Or at least I couldn't remember them doing so. And he said, 'If they don't have fingerprints, you don't have to stay here. I've seen a lot of people suffering in Italy, you know, without, like, accommodation, nothing.' And I said, 'I left my country to find a safe place to live. I didn't leave my country to live on the street. I'm not like that, I don't want to be like that.' So I had to carry on, moving forwards, to find, you know, a good country or something like that to look after me.

I kept moving till I got to Paris. Paris also has a lot of migrants. Thousands, you know. They sleep under bridges. I thought, 'What happened to them? Is it true? Is this really Europe?' People sleep under bridges and, you know, some people come and bring them food. It's like that. So again, I came to the realisation life is not easy here. A lot of people died, you know, trying to make the last step of the journey. Some people get caught under lorries and killed. But I thought, 'I've survived more risks than this. This is not going to be too difficult. This is normal for me. I have to try.' So I tried every day, every day, for a whole month. Then I got the chance. And I came.

Here

When I arrived in Dover, in 2012, they arrested me. The policemen took me to the station. Again I had problems with the language. They asked me, 'What language do you speak?' I understood they were asking me about languages, so I said, 'Arabic.' They got a translator and asked me, 'Why are you coming to the UK?' I said to them: 'I came to the UK to claim asylum; I am from Sudan.' They asked a few more questions, after which I stayed there for a day. The next day, immigration came. They asked me again my name, my date of birth, things like that. They asked me about the fingerprint again, and I said, 'I don't know.' Then they said, 'OK, you can have your fingerprint taken now.' And I went with them and they took it, and from there, from the police station, they took me to a detention centre. This was the first time.

From there they took me to another centre, near Dover. I stayed for, like, a week, and from there they released me to Manchester, to a hostel. I stayed there maybe one month and I got accommodation in Manchester. After that, one month, two months later, they sent me a letter. 'Your fingerprints are registered in Italy so you must claim your asylum there,' it said, plus a lot of other things. So I took the letter to a solicitor, who explained to me, 'Your fingerprints are registered in Italy so you must claim your asylum there. They have to talk with the Italians, and then, if they accept, they'll take you back to Italy. You have to go to the Home Office and sign in every two weeks.' And I said, 'All right.' There was a Home Office building just, like, ten minute's walk from my house. I went there two, three times. The fourth time, I didn't realise they were going to arrest me. I had left all my things at the hostel and just went there empty-handed. Someone started telling me: 'We're going to have to interview you.' And I said, 'Alright'. They took me to another room and locked the door. 'We're going to send you back to Italy,' they said.

From Manchester, they took me back to the first detention centre. I guess this was really my first proper time there. I stayed, maybe, four months. They gave me a voucher for using the TV, but I couldn't sit by myself. I had a solicitor but when I went into detention, they said, 'We can't help you in person because you're too far away.' 'OK,' I said, 'I'll just fight by myself.' After four months, I was released. They didn't take me back to Manchester; but gave me accommodation in Liverpool instead.

I stayed in Liverpool some time, and again they sent me a letter. I had to go to sign every two weeks, as before. So I went, maybe, a couple of times. After that, again they arrested me, and sent me back to the same detention centre. Again. This time I started to get to know the chaplain. I was sitting, you know, just eating my food, and he came over and asked me: 'Who are you? Where are you from? How long have you been here?' So we introduced ourselves and started to have a conversation. He asked me if I'd like any help. 'Yes, of course, I want help!' I said. 'Since I came to this country I've felt alone – nobody has helped me. I've been fighting by myself. Of course I want help!' I remember he put me in touch with a visitors group, and they started to ring me regularly. A woman, C came to visit me first. Then she came a second time. She was about to come a third time, when they deported me to Italy. You know, they came when I was asleep. Just, you know, sleeping. At three o'clock in the morning, they came in, maybe five people. They just opened the door, and woke me up. 'You're going to have to move,' they said. 'What's going on?' 'We're going to send you back to Italy today.' 'How?' I asked. 'Just, like that?' And they put handcuffs on me so I couldn't do anything about it, and took me back to Italy.

So now all my life had become like a dream. I start from the beginning.

I began to feel it was better to go back where I came from. I'm going to die here in Italy, I thought. It's better to die there. I thought, 'OK, I have two choices: go back to Sudan, to die there. Or try again to get to the UK. Because the only country I could be safe was there. I don't know how the Italians managed to take my fingerprints, or why they said I could claim asylum there. This is what I said to myself. I said, 'OK, I will try to go back to the UK.' Again, just like the first time, I tried, tried, tried.

And eventually I got here, where once again they arrested me in Dover. 'Who you are? Why you here?' I simply said the same I said the first time. Once more they took me to a detention centre. It was like the place was my home! Even the guards knew me. And, already knowing C, she found me a good solicitors company, and finally I started to get some help.

But, you know, in all this time I had forgotten my family completely. I had never forgotten them before. But ever since coming to Europe, I don't know how, I just started to forget about them. I was just thinking only about my own problems. I didn't know where they were or how they were and, they didn't know how I was or where I was, whether I was alive or not. So around this time I began to feel like giving up. I used to have strength. I used to have hope. But I had lost all this. I felt like my life had become very dark. My eyes were open but I could see nothing. I think I actually gave up.

But then I found my new solicitor, who was called John, and he started to work hard, asking many questions about my case. Soon after his first visit he brought a doctor from outside, someone from Medical Justice. She came to meet me in the detention centre, and saw from my body that I had been tortured in Sudan and Libya. Nobody previously had seen this. They just said things like, 'Your fingerprints are in Italy, we're going to send you there.' Nobody sat with me and listened to me. Nobody. They didn't understand what had happened to me. The only thing they cared about was the fingerprints, and all they said was, 'We're gonna send you back.'

John helped me a lot, and the doctor as well. She said because of my situation, I wouldn't be in detention more than one more day. I said to her, 'No one has ever sat with me and listened to me since I came here.' After that, maybe a week later, I was released. This time they didn't take me to Manchester, but to Leicester. Shortly after that they gave me accommodation in Derby. I was put in a room with another man. But, you know, I didn't care if it was two people to a room, or five, or ten, even if it was a small room. I felt like I was home finally and I just wanted to sleep.

You know, the first time I came to the UK, I had been so happy. I don't know why, but I felt so good, like a newborn baby. But after all these things that had happened to me, looking back at that time, I realised it was a fake happy. I was happy, but it wasn't right. I was happy with nothing, for no reason.

And after that, I remember, they brought me back to Leic ᵗer and sent me a letter saying I had an interview in C oventry. 'OK', I thought, 'I don't know what this one is about, but let's go.' I got there at nine o'clock in the morning and it went on until about two o'clock in the afternoon. It was a woman who interviewed me; she asked me, ah, hundreds of questions. Then she went right back to the beginning and asked the first question again. She wanted to make me confused. She asked the same questions all over again, and I was just … I was tired.

I had my interpreter with me, and he was getting tired too. Some of the questions I just answered, 'I don't know.' At which she said, 'How don't you know?' And she started asking me silly questions, like the things that had happened to my tribe; not to me, to my tribe, things before I was born. And when I shrugged, 'I don't know', she said, 'How come you don't know? It's your tribe.' And I said, 'I was never taught this – so how could I know?' After that I said, 'I give up, I can't do this anymore.' And she said, 'OK, we're finished now. Do you have anything to add?' I said, 'No, I don't have anything more to add.'

Following that I was waiting maybe a year and eight months, just for an answer, waiting for the result. I got another solicitor, because my old solicitor left the company. Eventually a decision was made: I was refused. But my new solicitor didn't tell me about my refusal. Instead, I got a bill for their services. I phoned C then I phoned my solicitor, and she said, 'Oh, you got a refusal a few days ago, and now we've sent you the bill.' C said, 'OK, we'll have to find another solicitor in Leicester.'

So when I came to Leicester, I met my fourth solicitor and she said, 'OK, first of all, we have to stop your previous appeal. You don't have time.' She stopped it and said, 'OK, we have to have an interview with you.' And she started from the beginning, like *really* from the beginning – like this account I'm giving you now. Since I arrived here, no one had asked me questions like hers. I started with when I was born. And after a while she said, 'I can defend you, because I know you, and I've got to know your case.' She worked hard, submitted a new appeal, and we won. So everything's alright.

If I were to compare my life here with the one I had in Sudan, there are a lot of differences. In Sudan people have a difficult life. We never feel safe. But when I lived around my family, I felt happy. I can see everything in front of my eyes, you know. Some people die, some people get shot, I witnessed the fighting. But I felt like I was OK because my mental health was fine. The problem here is – here, everything is safe, but it feels different, here everything is playing with my mind. I feel all the time my brain is working like a machine, it never stops. Everything plays with my thoughts. In my country, I would sleep well, and I would eat well – I love food. But since I came here, I don't eat much. I can't sleep. That's the difference between Sudan and here.

I heard that you had human rights in the UK, but where are those rights? Sometimes, they make me feel I'm a criminal – like when they put me in detention. I knew nothing about detention before I got here. Life in detention is, really, completely different. It is no life in detention. You don't know if it's the day or the night. Everything seems longer, even the days and the hours. In total, I have spent eight or nine months in detention, something like that.

And if you compare detention with prisons, it is strange to say but prison is better than detention. Why do I say that? Because in detention, you don't know how long it's going to last. It could be months, years, ten years, who knows. You don't know if you're going to be released or not. Some people live there maybe three years, then get deported back to their country. Sometimes, I would forget my situation completely. Seriously, that's what detention does to you. Some people in there are, like, disabled, and others have got much bigger problems than me. But no one cares about their problems. Seriously, that's detention. It's like, as they say, the worst time.

Finally, I have to say, I got my leave to remain. Finally. But, you know, when I got it, I didn't feel happy the way I did the first time I arrived, because something had died. Now all I can do is try to forget the things that happened to me. It's not easy, but I'm trying. Before I got my leave to remain, I remember I said, 'If you keep on being like that, one day you will lose your mind. You'll become crazy. You need to communicate with people, get to know others. You have to let people know about you, and your story.' I got the idea from the group I joined, which is Refugee Tales. Since I joined I have walked with people and I started thinking: 'I need to join with people.' So when I came back from their first walk, I started to volunteer. I am doing that now.

On Tuesdays, I volunteer with children and families; new arrivals to the UK. We have cooks and some of the volunteers, we play with the children. Some children want to play football, and we have space for that. We also have table tennis and a pool table. They say when they're in their hostel they feel like they're in prison, because they've not got anything to do there. They're happier when they come here, and when they realise we are like them, refugees like them.

I also volunteer on Fridays. I feel, you know, I would like to help other people. And even if it's not with my hands, I can speak. That's what I feel and that's what I'm doing now. So now I feel, like, you know, I am surrounded by a new family. I can feel that now. And I hope everything stays like that.

The Embroiderer's Tale

as told to

Patrick Gale

AND YES. SO I know this is not correct English grammar. I know not to begin every sentence with, 'And yes,' but they are such good words. And: promising there will be more. Yes: a smile in word form, quite different from its equivalent in Farsi, lifting the corners of the mouth, a handshake, a nod, an arm swept open in hospitality. And yes.

So please humour me. After Italy, which I might tell you about later, I find I reach for the good words, even when they don't make perfect sense. England is another good word, I am coming to see, like 'cake' and 'walk'.

Since I left home, I have learned several things besides English. I have learned that hospitality offered by strangers is a thing beyond the majesty of palaces. I have learned that dogs can be friends. And I have come to see that to have spotless hands is a luxury above feasting.

And yes, I am Iranian, from Tehran. My father and grandfather and great grandfather were tailors. Iranian men, as I'm sure you've noticed, if you pay close attention to the news, dress extremely conservatively, but they have a weakness for a well-chosen cloth and a crisply turned hem. I was trained as a tailor too. We had so much work that my father ran one workshop and I ran a second, from not long after I left school.

I was young to be in charge of people, but I was confident and had their respect because I was a good tailor. I *am* a good tailor. Hand me a bolt of winter-weight wool or a flash of summer-weight silk and my fingers can immediately tell how best to cut it, how best to make it hang from the shoulders, what thread to use with it, what buttons. To my eyes, most Englishmen dress like overgrown children, all colour but no shape.

I was a good boy. Dutiful. I went to mosque to say my prayers, honoured the Prophet, praised his Holy Name, and I pleased my father and mother. My mother was pious and I did nothing to upset her. I read no books other than school books, avoided the Internet, listened only to the singers she approved and never went to the cinema. My one indulgence, which she encouraged me in (because, I think, she secretly liked the sight of fit men's legs, even when only glimpsed from behind her chador) was football. I had clever feet – as accurate with a ball as my fingers were with a needle – and played often.

And yes, then I met Maryam. I'd be lying if I didn't admit that there have been many times since when I wished I had never met her. I would still be in Tehran with my family, probably married and a father by now because my mother and aunts were already starting to plan and plot which girl would best suit me.

But thanks to what Maryam started, I have come to see that there is a reason for things. Timothy, the man I live with now, has a framed postcard above his downstairs loo, which says, 'You came not to this place by accident.'

She was an Armenian. I could tell that from her surname even before she arrived for work. But I am not prejudiced like my mother; I am a craftsman and respect skill.

I set her the usual test, to unpick a seam and resew it along a line marked with chalk. She did this swiftly and neatly; I could hardly see the stitches.

'What else can you offer us?' I asked.

She looked at me solemnly and said, 'I can do invisible mending.'

'Show me,' I said.

So she said, 'Tear something, please.'

I tore a hole in the fabric she had just sewn, a jagged hole, like you'd get on barbed wire, and she took out a needle and reel of translucent thread from her own very neat little sewing kit, and in ten minutes it was hard to tell the hole had been there. And yes, I hired her.

She was a good worker and it was interesting because the other women who worked for me, all Muslim, all veiled, were far noisier than her, always chatting and gossiping and complaining as they worked, as though their veils were thick walls behind which they could say whatever they liked. But Maryam, sitting beside them, was... What's the word? There's a lovely English word, like the softest virgin wool. Demure. She was *demure*: eyes downcast, quiet, sometimes smiling to herself at the other women's stories as she stitched.

When her first pay day came, I praised her work and asked her if she was enjoying the job and she ducked her head and said, 'Yes. Thank you, yes.' But she looked at me briefly, with those eyes that were green like new greengages, not the cow-brown of everyone in my family. And yes, when her next pay day came, she lingered behind the others to be last in the queue. As she took her pay packet, she said her uncle, who she lived with because she was an orphan, would like me to come for supper, to thank me for employing her.

So I went.

I told my mother I was playing football and my football friends that I had a family party, and I went. Her uncle lived in an old house with a courtyard filled with lemon trees around a blue-tiled fountain. It was a special day for them, to celebrate Easter.

And yes, as we ate and they explained and Maryam told me stories, I fell in love with her. As easily as pulling on a glove. She was relaxed, not like at work, because she was with her family. She smiled a lot and her smile was peach-sweet and ticklish so that I had to make an effort to look at anyone else in the room.

As the meal reached the sweetmeat course I realised more people had arrived. The uncle ran a secret church, what Iranians call a house church, and these weren't born Christians, like Maryam, but secret ones, from Muslim families. They were what my mother called apostates.

'Will you join us?' Maryam asked. 'At midnight it will be Easter.' She smiled and said, 'There'll be special cakes,' and yes, I saw how much she trusted me because one word from me and these men and women would have been arrested.

So I stayed for the service in the church, which was in a sort of cellar in the oldest part of the house, where candles lit the vaulted ceiling and it was beautiful, perhaps especially because it was hidden, like a beautiful woman under her chador.

As Maryam saw me to the door afterwards, she kissed me swiftly on the cheek and said, 'Happy Easter and God bless you.' The kiss, the hint of her perfume and the strangeness of hearing myself say, 'Happy Easter,' back left me feeling so dizzy that I drove home without remembering what to say in answer to my mother's questions and my vague replies probably made her suspicious.

And yes. I went back. Of course I did. My other life, attending to my business, going to Friday prayers with my father, playing football with my friends, became like a fabric left too long in the sun.

Maryam admitted she loved me but said I would have to become a Christian for us to marry. It hadn't even occurred to me that I could do either of these. So I was baptised in her uncle's secret church. She kissed me on the lips that time, and gave me a bible of my own. And although we could only be ourselves at her uncle's house, our murmured exchanges over her sewing at work were now charged like a woman's eyes when the rest of her face is covered.

I began to dream of how we could move to Lebanon, perhaps, to be together, or to Egypt. Crazy dreams, I see now, but I was in love and lovers are slightly mad.

And yes, it all went wrong, as rapidly as a bolt of silk sliding off a table when you forget to weight it down.

I was playing football with my cousins and some friends. It was a warm evening and I was doing well. I'd scored three goals. The pitch floodlights made the city around us disappear, made the pitch feel like a stage where nothing could be hidden. None of my friends knew about Maryam and me; it was too dangerous. I kept it next to my heart, like the little silver crucifix she gave me.

Suddenly the little boy from next door was there, beside the pitch on his bike. He lived on that bike, running errands, spreading gossip.

'Hey, Mahdi!' he shouted out, for everyone to hear. He was grinning. For a moment I grinned back. 'Your mother has gone crazy and called the police. She found a bible under your pillow.'

Everyone stopped playing. One of my cousins cursed the the boy but my best friend, Parvaz, knew at once it was serious. 'You can't stay here,' he said quietly. 'They'll know you're here.'

So I ran and I drove to Maryam's uncle's house. I don't know how but they had already heard. Maryam wasn't there. There was no time to wait. Her uncle gave me a fleece and some long trousers in case I got cold later and bundled me into a car for the border. I had my ID card but no passport and no money. I was well off. If I'd been able to go to a bank, I'd have had money, but I was in sports clothes and I had nothing. Her uncle said he was paying and not to worry.

'God will provide,' he said.

He had paid an agent, he said, then he pressed a bag of food and drink into my arms and an envelope with Euros in it. I had never travelled. I didn't know if it was a little money or a great deal.

The driver wouldn't talk. He said it was safer that way, so we learned nothing about each other. He just drove and played music. Drove and drove. At some point late at night, he turned off the main road then on to a track and drove on with his lights off, using the moonlight, which scared me, but he said it was safest as we were near the border. Suddenly he stopped in the dark to check his phone. He read a text and flashed his headlights just once. Nearby some more lights flashed. We got out. In the moonlight I saw it was a lorry under the trees.

'Welcome to Turkey,' the man said. He told me to piss against a tree because it was a long journey then he helped me climb into the back by shining his torch. It was all crates of fruit. Oranges and tomatoes, I think. The scent was strong. And, in the middle, a little mattress.

I sat on the mattress and he pushed the crates so I was hidden. Then we drove.

I didn't think I would sleep because of the noise and the smell, and the worry of falling fruit boxes, but I did and I lost all sense of time in the darkness. I wondered if this was all a big mistake but then I realised there was no point even having the thought, as I had no more power to stop the lorry than the oranges and tomatoes did.

At one point, I woke when the back of the van was opened up and I heard the driver talking to another man in a language I didn't understand, Turkish maybe. And then I woke because we had driven on to a boat. The lorry was rocking this way and that and I was sick under the mattress. I felt bad about that.

Soon after, we drove off the boat and the driver let me out. He said we were in Italy now so I was safe. 'But don't give your fingerprints or you have to stay here always,' he said, 'And we were paid to get you to England.'

Then he drove one way while I had to walk another and join a queue of people on foot.

And yes, I showed my card and remembered to smile and look the men in the eye because Italy is a Christian country and I'd be safe there. But something was wrong. They shouted at me and they pulled me out of the queue and put me in a truck with some men from Africa, everyone frightened, everyone talking in languages I didn't know. They drove us to a police station and shut us in cells.

My cell was cupboard small. It was hot with no fresh air and no mattress, just a hard bench. If I needed the loo, I had to call out and beg. They took me to a place with no door and no sink and not always paper. I have never felt so dirty. When they brought me food, it was bread and cheese, so I had to eat with my filthy hands and I worried I'd get sick.

I was there for days. Nobody spoke Farsi, only Italian. Sometimes they tried English but I only knew a few words.

'*Firma qui!*' they kept saying. 'Sign!' but what they wanted was my fingerprints and I wouldn't.

Eventually I cracked, anything to get out, even though I was scared about having to stay somewhere so bad. So I let them take my fingerprints and suddenly they were all smiles and shrugs and they put me out on the street. I washed my hands and face in a very cold fountain and even drank from it then went into a church to pray. After that, I sat on a bench outside the police station to wait.

Eventually a driver stopped. He knew my name. He had been coming by every day at the same time. He had no Farsi but he had a sheet of paper with phrases copied out from the Internet in different languages I could point to. So once he knew my language, he pointed to *You can call me Piero* and *I have been paid to take you to France* and *No more borders until England!*

He was driving a minibus. We drove to a multistorey car park and picked up more people. Women and men and some children as well. At first, nobody spoke except the ones who were travelling together. Everyone was tense, especially when the driver saw a policeman and flapped his hand and shouted, 'Giu! Giu!' till we all dropped on the floor out of sight. It was like that all the way to France. Sometimes we'd relax and people would sing or try sign language and it would start to feel like the strangest holiday, then we'd see policemen with guns and everyone would fall silent and hide behind the minibus's ragged orange curtains.

When we stopped to let the driver rest or to get food or relieve ourselves, you could tell we were all scared of being left behind. Nobody spoke Farsi so I felt very alone in the group. I worried they'd forget me and I'd be stranded on the motorway. By the time we were in France, most people had left to get into other vans. We drove into a big forest as the sun was sinking.

Piero said something serious, then handed me to some other men. They checked my identity card and asked lots of questions I couldn't understand. They weren't friendly; they were frightened. There was nothing to eat.

And yes, they made me sleep in a tiny tent with several other men. One wouldn't stop crying, even when the others shouted at him. I think someone had died.

We woke hearing a lorry arrive. They made us get into packing cases, wooden ones. They pointed at the air holes, making panting noises to explain, and then handed us each a plastic bottle of water and an empty one. Rude gestures showed what the empty ones were for. They sealed us in and loaded us into the lorry among cases which had other things in them. Not people. I am not scared of the dark. Not very. But I am tall and used to moving all the time. If you get cramp when you can't stretch your leg out straight, it hurts.

I lost track of time because of the darkness. And my phone battery was dead so I had no light. Once again we went on a boat. This time I wasn't sick, maybe I was empty. We arrived somewhere and the lorry started up again. I was sure we would be checked. I was sure I would soon hear shouts and splintering wood but no, we just drove for maybe two hours. We stopped at last and I could hear packing cases being ripped open at last. People talking in their languages.

'Hemel Hempstead,' a man was saying, quite angrily. 'Hemel Hempstead. England. Go. Go now!'

That's what he said to me when it was my turn to be let out. 'Go. Hurry!' But my legs were so cramped I could barely move so he had to help me down to the ground before he drove quickly away. We were in a car park in a town. It was night. Street lights in the distance and a big road.

I found myself on a normal street with takeaways and shops. It was busy with traffic and people, so I could disappear like a thread in thick felt. I tried not to stare at everything. I was worried I must smell bad and look wild.

I heard a man and woman speaking Farsi. And yes, it was so surprising I smiled – although they were arguing – and he saw and broke off to say, 'Hello, my friend.'

'Hello,' I said.

The woman looked suspicious and told him, 'We'll be late,' but he looked kindly at me and said,

'You've just arrived, haven't you?'

'Yes,' I said.

'Do you have friends here?' he asked. 'Family?'

'No,' I told him. So he wrote down his number, although the woman was clucking at him like an angry hen.

'Ring me,' he said. 'Arsham. You have one friend here now.'

I tucked his card with my money in my sock and tried to buy some food, but they wouldn't take my money as it was Euros and then there was a policewoman beside me, holding my elbow.

Every traveller here, every refugee, has their own story as different as they are. The trouble is that all the stories become the same in the same way because they all, sooner or later, narrow down to a lorry, a box, a cell.

They said it wasn't prison. When they finally found me someone who could speak Farsi, she explained it was a detention centre for people like me with nobody to vouch for us.

I explained to her. I left nothing out apart from the fingerprints in Italy because I was scared of being sent all the way back there, and about Arsham, because I kept thinking of his wife and how impatient she looked as he gave me his number. He looked kind but she was dressed like my mother. I knew she would think me an apostate.

But they kept asking. 'Who can you ring? Who do you know?'

The detention centre, near a big airport, was nicer, I think, than a prison. There were plenty of meals and the beds weren't uncomfortable. But it felt like prison because we couldn't leave and because the women and men were kept in different parts, like in a mosque. There were good things there: I could play football every day in the yard like a cage, which helps when you all speak different languages, and I could go to a chapel and be as Christian as I liked. I started to learn English properly. Every day.

But there were bad things, too: the boredom, the feeling idle and the violence. And football or suppertime could turn into a fight.

I had dreams that woke me up sweating and shouting so that people shouted back or thumped on the door. I found it hard not to cry, especially in the chapel. I went, not just for God but because it was quiet and empty. When I started to cry, I found it hard to stop.

So finally I said, 'Yes. OK. Yes. I have a friend called Arsham I can ring.' So they gave me a phone and said ring him and I took the paper with his number and I prayed in my head and when he answered I laughed and laughed because I was so happy it wasn't his angry wife. And yes, he knew at once who I was and very calmly, like a wise mullah, said let me speak to them.

He was very good. And so was Shideh, his wife, even though she didn't want me there. Maybe she was especially good because she didn't want me there.

I slept in their spare room for eight whole weeks. I tried to give them all my money but Arsham only took it to turn it into pounds for me. They fed me, they took me to the library so I could read and have more English lessons from a lady like a grandmother who was not paid but said she did it *for love*. And they made sure I did not forget the days when I had to go a long way on the train and bus to sign the form for the police and answer questions I was beginning to understand. And, kindest of all, because they were both Muslims, they took me to the door of the local church.

In church I made friends, especially Timothy, who vouched for me when I was taken back to the detention centre when I forgot to sign in one week because I was ill and crying in my room. And yes, Timothy took me in and gave me his spare room and said I could live there free of charge while he helped me to claim asylum.

He has helped in so many ways. He realised I needed to work, although I am not allowed to earn money, so he gave me his dead wife's sewing machine and I started mending and altering clothes for charity and helping mend vestments at the church.

One day he saw me working on an altar front, a very old one, where the pattern had been eaten by moths and needed a repair. I was puzzling over it because it was not the sort of sewing I knew how to do. He taught me two new words on the spot and wrote them down for me on the little pad we use: *Tapestry* and *Embroidery*. Embroidery can also mean making up stories, or making stories better, which I like very much. He showed me pictures on the Internet. When I liked a tapestry that looked like a painting but all in silk, he said, 'Oh, we can go and see that easily.'

And he took me to the palace at Hampton Court and explained its history – most of which I didn't understand but he told me anyway because his wife was dead and he needed to talk and tell stories. The tapestries there were so big, with figures bigger than life-size and so very beautiful. I made him laugh because he tried to show me the rest of the palace and the gardens, which are beautiful and strange, but I kept asking when we could see the tapestries again.

'Would you like to learn?' he asked. 'Men can learn as well as women.'

So I said, 'Yes. Yes, please.' And he signed me up for a course at the Royal School of Needlework.

We learn high up in the attics of the palace. And yes, I am usually the only man there but I don't mind because the ladies are very kind and tell me I have a gift, like I did for football. If the detention centre was a kind of hell, the needlework school is like a kind of heaven, and not just because it's up in the clouds. The rooms are all painted white so the rainbow walls of glass drawers where you can see all the coloured wools and silks waiting are all the brighter. It is quiet, because we concentrate so hard as we sew tiny flowers and leaves and birds, and it is calm, like the calmest summer's day with no wind, and oh so clean, because we are encouraged to wash our hands many times a day to keep the fabric unmarked.

I made a red rose for my first exercise, using more reds than I can hold in my mind's eye and I thought it was full of mistakes, but all the ladies gathered around when I finished and made sounds like doves in a warm courtyard.

They want me to stay. They want me to do exams so that I can teach. And yes, they want me to tell them my story. But I only tell small parts, here and there, because it makes me too sad.

The sadness is bad. Timothy took me to see a doctor about it because some days it was like a heavy cloud pressing down on the bed stopping me getting up. And I was given pills and they help a bit. But they don't stop the bad dreams and memories. Of the trucks. Of the forest. Of Italy.

So Timothy made me choose a dog in a place like a detention centre for dogs, a terrible place full of sadness and wild barking. Tina is small and very bristly and brown, with eyes the colour of caramel. He says she is a mongrel but I think that sounds ugly so I just call her Tina. He says she is ours, but I know she is really mine because I walk her and feed her and brush her. She seems to have chosen me, he says, because she sleeps outside my room, very close to the door. And if I wake with the sad cloud over me, she knows and pushes and licks my toes and fingers and ears until I get up to walk her. She is better than a pill. And yes, I hold her close, although we were told never to touch dogs at home, and she makes me feel better. She makes me feel now, rather than then.

Timothy says I can ring my mother to tell her I am all right and I nearly have a few times. But then I remember that she called the police when she found my bible. He asks if I want to ring Maryam, if I miss her badly. And yes, I nearly do but Maryam seems so far away now, like a tiny figure in a picture on a wall in a big gilt frame. Sometimes I think Maryam was like an angel, mysteriously taking jobs around Tehran to make Muslim boys fall in love with her and become Christian. I think she will be working somewhere else now shyly saying thank you to a boy who can't stop looking at her in the hope of catching her eye.

Instead I try to be like Tina, and think only of now. And tomorrow. My next embroidery. Our next walk by the Thames.

I wash my hands whenever I can. Timothy has Pears soap, which is brown and smells of spices and leather. The soap at the needlework school smells of lavender. I sniff my fingers and smell only soap. If I look straight ahead, or down at Tina's caramel eyes or closely at the blue and purple stitches beneath my fingers, life is good.

And.

Yes.

The Dancer's Tale

as told to

Lisa Appignanesi

I KNOW IT'S YOU before we meet. Even though the appointed entrance hall is vast and tiered and crowded with people whose movements, as they approach and leave the security desks, I watch from my perch at the corner café.

Yet you don't look like a refugee. You are calm. You are erect and perfectly poised as you balance on a stool near a window. I must be wrong, I tell myself. I scan the hall once more.

I have come early to observe from a distance. There is plenty of time to interrogate my own perceptions. What do I actually think a refugee looks like?

Harrowing images of women and babies on sinking boats leap into my mind; a tattered, angry mass at the Jungle in Calais; children behind barbed wire fences; clamouring groups in tented cities.

I realise that with all my good intentions, I inhabit a realm of stereotype created by news images, mostly depicting groups in situations of terror – all that compounded with the extract of Emma Lazarus' 1883 poem on the Statue of Liberty:

> Give me your tired, your poor,
> Your huddled masses yearning to breathe free,
> The wretched refuse of your teeming shore…

Masses, yes, but no individualised image of a refugee comes into my mind. A visual and literary rhetoric that conjures up hordes has usurped the place of the person.

Yet my whole family were refugees from a war-torn Europe that turned stereotypes and labels into killing decrees. It is specific features I remember them by, not a group designation. I know their faces better than my own, just as I know individual attributes, say, of the German/Jewish philosopher Theodor Adorno, who fled Nazi race laws to find a home in America; – or of Voltaire and Rousseau who took refuge from silencing tyrannies in Britain.

Refugees are a multiplicity of individuals, ordinary and extraordinary, wrenched by circumstance from homes that have become uninhabitable, tossed about in the endless paperwork that nation states engender – ever more so in the age of the computer that proliferates quantifiable categories but has little place for the complexities of the human heart.

My musings have taken me away from you. I glance your way again, not wanting to be too obvious. What is it about you that makes me think it is *you* I am here to meet? You sit tall, straight, very still, with a sculptural poise. Your hands are in your lap. They move only occasionally in graceful gestures I can't read from my distance. Your head is held high beneath a dark bristling crown of hair. Your youth is evident in your features. Your dark eyes are older, eloquent.

I realise it is because I have been told you are a dancer that I have singled you out. In my mind, the designation 'dancer' trumps any received image of 'refugee'.

It is time. I move towards the information desk, take out my phone and punch out the number I have been given. I see the man you are with pick up his. I smile. Across the room you do, too. We have both, I will learn in a few minutes, recognised each other from our professional habits: writers, you tell me, observe. We give ourselves away just as much as dancers do by their poise. This, I feel, is a better use of identities, than the others we sometimes adopt.

When we have reached the space where we will talk and have set the recorder in train, you begin to tell me your story. Your English is good. Very soon this pleasant room with its bustle of others disappears and we are in the north of Sri Lanka where your childhood unfurled. It was a fulfilled childhood until the ongoing civil war came too close. You had everything. A sister who was three years older, a loving mother who looked after you both and taught you how to be strong as well as how to share your feelings and hold on to your opinions.

You don't remember meeting your father until you were about ten. Threats had forced him outside the district the civil war had shunted you to in search of safety. You were in town. He worked for the government with small groups of Tamils elsewhere. He was Catholic, your mother Hindu. Ever present, ever ready to listen to anything you wanted to confide, and ever in your eyes utterly heroic, she so arranged things that you didn't even really miss your absent father. In fact, you didn't even really know the country was at war.

At first you were sent to a convent school and then in the fifth grade to a boys' school. You were very young when you started to dance. Your older sister had lessons and she learned by practicing with you. She needed someone to teach and, in this case, you were all too willing to comply.

One day, while you were at school, a bomb blast rocked the building. You hid under the table. All of you did. The blasts continued. Then your mother appeared and shepherded you through streets filled with tumult and rubble and the dark green and black of army uniforms. Everyone was shouting amidst the noise of blasts. You could feel rage and fear in the streets. And you, too, as you were rushed first towards your sister's school and then home by your brave mother, were frightened. The war which had only been a rumour was now everywhere and also inside you.

Huddled at home, you began to listen to the news. There was tension in the family. Your mother thought you might all have to move again. She rang your father for advice. Your grandmother had already lost one son to war. Old stories were retold, though this was the first time you remembered hearing them and feeling their emotional charge. You began to learn about the LTTE – the Liberation Tigers – the struggle for independent Tamil nationhood, the shifts and sways in control between government and Tamil forces in various parts of the northern province. You began to understand that there was an onus on you to protect your land and culture and history.

When a temporary peace was cobbled together, you went back to school. The curriculum was centralised. History was Singhalese history, though everything was taught in Tamil. But the Tigers came to the school and taught you an alternate history, that of the ancient Tamil people. They also said students should aspire to do all kinds of studies, become doctors and lawyers. Martyr days were held, filled with performance. You loved this – the dance and music and storytelling. You wanted to participate. You didn't at all think of it as a means of fighting against the government, certainly not anything associated with killing. It was a way of communicating Tamil values, and as your grandmother was pleased to note, paying tribute to your uncle.

I stop you and ask what Tamil values are. Tamil, for you, means all the countless ancient stories your grandmother tells, the songs and performances, the language itself with its sounds that are like feelings. When you speak it you are at home. English is a second skin. Now part of you, but still second, like Singhalese too, which you learned on holidays when you went to stay with your father.

By the time you were doing your O and then A levels, you were also travelling the Northern and Eastern province, where most Tamils live, as a performer. Not all children were lucky enough to be able to afford an education, so the performances – the dance, that combined movement, music and storytelling – served as an education in Tamil traditions. Some of your friends joined the Tigers. They asked you to join, but you didn't.

When your mother found out you were missing classes to perform, she was furious. She slapped you. She didn't want you involved in politics. You tried to say what you were involved in was art, but she would have none of it. She told you to get your head back into your studies and nothing else.

And then everything changed again. The Tigers had to move out of your area and the Army moved into town. A curfew was instituted. Shops were closed. All activities stopped early. Fear and suspicion permeated the atmosphere. It was 2009 and the war was at its peak. People were disappearing. They never returned. No one could be trusted. There was a terror of informers.

While you waited for your A level results in the hope that they would be good enough to get you out of the war zone to a university in the eastern province, one of your mother's friends asked if you could do some volunteering work with Handicap International, an NGO that was working in the region together with the UN. You had some English and could translate, and you knew something about first aid.

Every day the UN brought injured people to the Handicap headquarters. The queues started at 6.30 in the morning and by the time you arrived a little later they tailed back for ever. The stories people told were horrendous. There was blood everywhere… missing limbs, contorted faces.

You look away from me. I see that you have begun to play with the ties of your red sweatshirt, winding and winding them, as if you were making rope.

You go on, mumbling over the worst. You remember a tall boy, about your own age and wearing a yellow T-shirt who couldn't sit his exams, because his injury made it impossible for him to sit. He wanted a special chair. He asked for books.

Your voice wanders off. After a moment you tell me that at the end of this period, you had a breakdown. You wanted to work, you wanted to learn more English, you wanted to help, but you had started to cry unstoppably. You couldn't eat. You could barely get out of bed, though it was also the site of nightmares.

One day when you had gone to sit in the library, your mother had threatening visitors. They described you, described what you were wearing – a particular red T-shirt and jeans. They had their eyes on you, they said. They were watching. You were sent away to hide at an uncle's for a few days.

On 10th July, it was your sister's birthday. There was no real celebration, since your father who often came for these birthdays, couldn't get into town, but your mother was preparing dinner for you all. You were sitting at your computer, when the front gate rattled and shouts erupted. You could see a van on the street in front of the house. Your mother went and told whoever it was to go away.

Then two men burst in. They were wearing masks. Their guns pointed at the three of you. One put his gun to your head and wrestled you to the floor, twisting your arms behind your head.

When you woke up there was a blindfold over your eyes. You could smell rot and dust, hear weeping and pleading voices. Soon you knew the worst. You were in a military camp filled with detainees – the disappeared.

As you talk about this, cursorily, briefly, you look away from me again. You are very still, while your hands twist and twist the cord on your top into a rope.

You can still smell the blood you tell me. You were raped. Regularly. And tortured. They kicked you around like a ball. They wanted information. They interrogated you about the Tigers. Someone, you didn't know who, had informed on you. You were in a state of perpetual pain and terror.

I am about to pose another question when I realise I am repeating the act of interrogation. I have a vision of you going through the asylum procedures, the endless questioning, the appeals and interrogations. You must experience these as repetitions of those traumatic times, this time enacted by a bureaucracy that is meant to be benign. Yet all its apparatus calls up terror.

I still my questions and wait.

You don't know how you survived, you say, after a few moments. Perhaps it was the image of your mother, her aura of strength.

You were in the camp for about six months. Then your father managed to organise your escape. You still don't know exactly how he did it, but it seems he talked to one of the Tamil groups that supported the government and they helped to locate you. He paid them money. You were almost dead when they got to you: you couldn't walk or talk or open your eyes properly, but they blindfolded you in any case and dumped you in the midst of some wild forest.

From there you were taken to a doctor friend: you couldn't go to a hospital. It would have betrayed too much of the government's doings and endangered you further. But you had nonetheless to report to the police every month and promise that you would never leave Sri Lanka. Meanwhile your father was in touch with friends in London and attempting to get you a visa. You didn't know this. You didn't want to go. All you wanted to do was be at home, safe with your family. When the visa came through, you couldn't bear to leave. You felt you were losing your studies, your family, your future, your body, your very soul. You said you would rather die in Sri Lanka.

But the agency your father had paid spirited you off to Colombo and put you on a plane. By then, you had ceased to feel anything. Perhaps you were in shock. Certainly you never talked about what had happened to you to the family you were lodged with in London. To mention torture was shaming. You stayed silent. There was no talking about such matters. Then, too, it was impossible to trust anyone, even here.

You had to go to college. You were on a student visa. Yet you felt completely lost. There was nothing you wanted to study. Nothing you wanted to do. Then you learned from your mother that your sister had disappeared on her way to work. You started to cry and couldn't stop. You locked the door of your room and tried to hang yourself.

You have been knotting the cords of your shirt again and now I see them as hanging rope. I wait, then prod you into the present with my words.

Yes, the lady of the house stopped you. She quizzed you. You told her about your sister. There were phone calls.

Luckily nothing terrible, beyond interrogation – in part about you – happened to your sister. And with money, your father once more managed to obtain a release. Your sister was in a state of shock and it was thought best that she move out of town. Your father at this point was working for the irrigation department in an area relatively unaffected by war. There were women's quarters there and your sister was taken in.

When peace was declared, you wanted to go home. You missed your family dreadfully. You couldn't understand why you still felt so ghastly, so lost. There was no one you could talk to.

Your mother phoned and said you mustn't come back. Whatever the declarations of peace, it wasn't the right time to come home. There might be an abatement of war, but people were still being snatched and disappeared. After your sister had been kidnapped, she felt unable to go out in the streets alone, since she might be grabbed by the army.

After that phone call, you really didn't know what to do. You didn't want to stay here, yet you couldn't go back. Instead you walked. And walked some more. You held the pain inside yourself. You found yourself at the Ealing Temple and you prayed to Shiva, walking round his statue, as custom dictates, and trying not to cry. But you were crying in any case, or so you found when a man addressed you, asked if you were all right, whether you'd like some of the lunch that was on offer inside. You felt you needed someone to save your life: neither food nor meditation could do that.

You left and started to walk again. This time your feet took you to a church in Wembley. It was closed but there was a statue of Mary outside, and seeing the statue reduced you to tears. Now you couldn't stop crying. You prayed for direction. It grew dark and still you were there. Then you started walking once more and found yourself back at the Temple with its meditation centre and the same man was standing there. Once more he offered help. You couldn't speak for weeping. And despite his evident kindness, you still couldn't summon up the trust to open up.

Perhaps the man guessed your state. He said he could direct you to people in the Red Cross who might be able to help you, to whom you could talk. He suggested you visit a Centre in the north of the city. You went, were lucky to get an appointment for the next day. That was when you learned that given what you had been through, and the danger of return, you could apply for asylum. You would need a solicitor and legal aid. That could be found through the meditation centre.

However beguiling the word asylum, a new ordeal was about to start. Whenever you told your story to the authorities, you were asked for concrete proof: if you were raped, if you were tortured, where was the evidence? If you were released, where was the document testifying to your release? Not being believed, being re-interrogated, is its own form of torture. Asylum was refused.

You were devastated. You were told to appeal. The barrister never made it to court, and when you agreed to speak through an interpreter, you found that the Tamil interpreter didn't like your accent: his was so dusty, he must have picked it up in some arcane London library. Are you really a Tamil, you were asked? You turned to the judge and said you would try to explain to him directly in English. There was no immediate ruling on the appeal. You carried on reporting to the border police every week, each time holding your breath. The booths, the chains, the police officers who couldn't talk to you in a normal way. They only shouted names and numbers, as if you were deaf, as well as stupid. Everything was names and numbers.

After the appeal, when you reported to the border police office, the police kept you waiting for hours. From 9am until

4pm, when you were at last called. They kept saying your case was being checked. After all that, at the end of the day, they announced you were now to be taken into detention. You didn't understand. You thought perhaps the Sri Lankan army had intervened. When you were told you could make a single phone call, you rang your caseworker at the Red Cross to tell him what had happened.

They pushed you into a van with two Afghanis. No one told you where you were headed. On arrival they snapped your picture and took all your possessions. You were in a state of terror. As if you were back in the prison camp and all the atrocities you had experienced there were to be replayed. You started panicking. They thrust you into a room. The man already in it was ill and couldn't stop coughing. They took him off to the hospital in the middle of the night. In the morning when the call came from the Red Cross, you begged them to come and fetch you. They said they couldn't make a bail application because you didn't have a solicitor. They asked whether they could share your information with a Sri Lankan campaign group that helped people detained in the UK. They would find you a lawyer.

When one turned up, once more you didn't know whether to trust him. But soon, he became the most important person in your life. He was your only link to the world outside. It was he who got in touch with a UN rapporteur who knew what had been happening to the Tamils in Sri Lanka. Gradually they put your case together.

Meanwhile you waited in the detention centre. There was no contact allowed with the outside world there, no email, nothing. It brought back memories of being in isolation in Sri Lanka. The guards were often brutal. And they were always there. Even when you were in the shower. You started to lose weight and hair. You couldn't swallow. They were about to pack you onto a plane and send you back to Sri Lanka: they didn't believe that it was a dangerous place for you. Your solicitor intervened and said you were too ill to be put on a plane.

One day a guard jumped you. He put his knees into the small of your back and tugged.

You show me the posture, curving your body on the chair you sit in, so that I can read the pain. Your eyes have grown darker.

After that you were thrust into isolation. You made another suicide attempt. There was just no point going on.

And then suddenly, after two and a half months in detention you were released. Your solicitor had worked hard to research all aspects of your case and he had triumphed.

Soon you would have asylum and leave to stay in the UK. But meanwhile your life felt increasingly fragile. When you went back to the family you had first stayed with, you were thin, pale and sick. They were very uncomfortable having you around. You didn't blame them. You were uncomfortable with you, too. But nor could you transform yourself.

You took up the offer of accommodation in a hostel. It was winter and cold. The evening of the day you arrived you didn't know what to do with yourself amidst the strange sounds that rose to your room – the noise, the banging, the sound of glass being thrown. You got out of bed and when you put your feet on the floor it felt oddly hot. You put your shirt on and opened the door. There was smoke everywhere, thick and so heavy you couldn't see through it. This was the end, you thought. Kannagi, the brave heroine of the ancient Tamil epic, *The Silappatikaram* or *The Story of the Anklet*, leapt into your mind: she had torched the city of the King who had wrongfully imprisoned her husband for theft.

But the man who had seen you arrive earlier in the day made his way through the smoke to rescue you. He was brave, even though he was in a state of desperation because he had been refused asylum.

Outside there were police and fire engines. It was freezing, despite the fire. When a mini cab driver offered you his jacket, you felt warmed by his gesture as well as by the coat. Amidst all the awfulness, there was some humanity, too.

You lost everything in that fire, your remaining clothes, your papers. But somehow those two gestures of help, plus the hope of your new status, gave you some strength.

You were now offered temporary accommodation in the far east of the city. There was another asylum seeker living in the house. One night, in a fit of drug induced madness, he started to attack you with a knife. You had to call the police.

Gradually things began to improve. The therapist helped. You started to put things together and get a little distance from the unspeakable parts of your past. At the detention centre you had been incapable of speech – one visitor characterised you as cowering under the bed and muttering gibberish. But now, now you had begun to speak.

Through your solicitor, you were introduced to a woman who ran a programme for seniors in a community centre. She asked you to help with dance classes. She too was a Bharathanatyam dancer.

The pleasure is evident in your face now as you talk of dancing and then tell me how you took up a photography programme in the local college, started to help regularly with elder care. You had wanted to do a course in health and social care, but it needed a work placement, and people didn't trust asylum seekers, thinking they might run away.

And then you were asked by a Tamil group to perform some storytelling dances for them. You experienced the dance as therapeutic. It was a place of expression, but also of safety. It touched the traumatic parts of your history. In dance, you seemed to be able to enact all the horrors you had been through and also triumph over them.

You mentioned this to the therapist you were seeing and she introduced you to the few courses on offer in dance psychotherapy. There were all these strong women around you again, like your mother had been. And when your refugee status wonderfully came through, you started to do a foundation course in dance psychotherapy at Goldsmiths'. Not only did you perform for a Bengali charity, but you did movement and meditation sessions with patients. You want to work: if you're home and alone you get too emotional.

When you're performing you feel like your whole body is purified. You use the Five Rhythms technique, now established as a form of dance movement therapy. It's based on the idea that everything is energy: the body in motion can be used to still the mind. You feel you started dancing in your mother's womb, and you're very grateful to her, and now want to share this world of energy and safety with others. You have plans to do a graduate degree in dance psychotherapy.

And now, now that your refugee status has come through, now that you've been in Britain for almost six years, you want to see your mother. You want to see her desperately – but she and your father agree that a meeting still can't take place safely in Sri Lanka. You hope to arrange to meet her somewhere in India perhaps.

As you tell me this, I think to myself, you might want to dance for her.

The Care Worker's Tale

as told by

B

ALMOST 20 YEARS AGO, I was a student and a Fulani activist in the youth section of an opposition party of the Fulani people. I participated in, and was an organiser of, student demonstrations against the government, demanding the electrification of the city and the lowering of the price of petrol. The exorbitant increase of the price of petrol, which caused public and private transport to increase fares, had made getting to educational establishments impossible for ordinary and lower earning families. They simply could not pay for their children to get to school. The demonstration was staged for three consecutive days by all educational establishments and activists in the capital city, which disturbed the running of all government institutions and businesses as demonstrators and the security forces battled for days. Scores of people were killed and detained by the security forces during these days of demonstration. As a Fulani activist, I was arrested and tortured, and put into prison for months without trial until I was temporarily released with restrictions on compassionate grounds. It was during this temporary release I escaped the country aided by an agent promising to get me to a safe place.

★

On my arrival in the UK, I claimed asylum. I told them who I was, my situation and what I had been through in my country. I was given temporary accommodation while they processed my application. After six months my application was refused despite all the overwhelming evidence I provided them with. As I was still a teenager when I arrived in this country, I was handed to social services who looked after me until 2004.

That year, following a visit to see a friend, I was arrested in Scotland and put into a detention centre for two weeks and then released. After my release, I went to the Refugee Council in Brixton to seek legal advice as I was released on temporary admission. I was advised by a woman there that my case was finished, that it was better for me to run or I would be deported. As I knew deportation was out of the question for me, because of the risks if I returned, I decided to hide with friends around the country. I was arrested in Dover trying to leave the UK and was sentenced to twelve months in prison with automatic deportation. I spent six and a half months in various prisons around the country and six and a half months in the Dover Immigration Removal Centre.

In prison, my plumbing tutor was a factor in motivating me and enabling me to see that everything is possible if you have determination and are willing to learn. He told me he left school at sixteen without a certificate and could not read or write a proper word because he was dyslexic. He said he learned plumbing and excelled, and then worked for over 40 years until he retired. One day, he said, he went to a school to demonstrate plumbing skills to pupils and after his demonstration the head of the school told him he should teach. Knowing that he was dyslexic, he told her that he could not because his spelling was very poor, but she told him everyone can do something in this world, that we all have different talents. He accepted the challenge and went on to do a teaching course at university and now he's a plumbing teacher with a university degree.

My intention was to do a plumbing course after my release as his story was an inspiration to me and he always used to tell me that he trusted me to achieve whatever I wanted to achieve. However, while in detention I got hooked on reading social sciences. I read philosophy, psychology, self-help and religious books. Reading those books transformed me and gave me a different understanding of life. I decided on my release I would try to do a psychology degree to help those who have different ways of coping in this world due to the challenges they face or have faced before. I wanted to be a counsellor or a social worker.

★

In Dover, I could not get a surety to get me out of the detention centre. I went for bail a few times but the judge kept asking me for a surety which I could not provide. Not until someone told me about a charity who linked detainees with people prepared to provide bail. I spoke to them but I had to wait for over two months as they told me it was difficult to find someone at that time. I stayed there until one day they called me to say they had found someone who was keen. At that point, I realised I had the best support network to get out of detention. My surety stood for me and within three weeks I was out of detention; my thirteen long months in detention were coming to an end.

After my release, I had to do what I said and achieve my goal of getting a degree. It was a challenge, with no formal academic education and having left school several years before. I started an access course in psychology, which was very demanding, but I finished the course and completed all my modules with either a pass or a merit. The biggest challenge, however, was getting into higher education. All my classmates had applied and been accepted by different universities across London. I couldn't apply because I wasn't eligible for student finance. But still, it was my goal to get a university degree. I started contacting organisations that could help on a daily basis, but this was around the end of August and they told me they could not offer a bursary as it was too late to enrol. Still, I just kept googling for organisations that help people like me get into higher education. I had nothing to lose but everything to gain.

Eventually, after many calls, I was given the number of the Helena Kennedy Foundation. I contacted them and they passed me the number of one of their sub-organisations called Article 26. I spoke to them and they said they would try to see if I could get a place at a university first. I asked them for a psychology place but they told me it was very unlikely as the psychology courses would be full. Instead I chose a management degree, for which I was offered a place at a university in London.

I had untold difficulties during my years of study thanks to the UKBA's constant threat of deportation and the prospect of my case being refused. I had financial problems as well, living a cashless life in London for over five years on a £35 weekly food voucher, made even more humiliating by many supermarkets asking you for your ID card or driving licence with every purchase. These difficulties accumulated, but I never gave up as I had a goal. I wanted to succeed through academic study and go on to contribute to society in any positive way I could.

Finally, after three years of university studies, I graduated. I then had to wait another year to win my appeal. Over a decade after I first sought asylum in the UK, I was granted a British Residence Permit (BRP). Immediately afterwards I had to leave my accommodation and find work. A week later, I started working in kitchens to sustain myself, to meet my rent, food and personal needs, as a temporary solution until I could figure out a suitable career or work for myself. I worked in the kitchen for nine months then left. I started asking friends about plumbing and gas engineering and spoke to many apprenticeship organisations, but I found that route was not feasible. I then decided to try care work, though I was worried my past conviction for an immigration offence would be an obstacle. My first contact with a care employment company was in the West Country. I told them about my offence, showed my DBS, and they told me it was not a problem. They trained me for a week but then for three months they kept turning me around, saying I was not suitable for the job. Their attitudes made me think I might not get into care work as I didn't know how the sector worked.

But I never gave up. I tried other care recruitment companies until one of them trained me and then offered work. For the past three years, I have been working, sometimes full-time, sometimes part time. I work with service users with learning disabilities, autism and dementia. I have found my life's purpose in these jobs. I love it. My fascination is to understand human behaviour and the job is the best job I have ever done in my life. I want to make a difference in other people's lives. It is rewarding and a blessing and it fills my soul with joy.

My mantra of not giving up, of refusing to fail, and the extraordinary support I receive from my friends, my university, Article 26 and other charities are the keys to my success. They gave me the motivation to push myself despite all the challenges I faced.

The Fisherman's Tale

as told to
Ian Sansom

You're not really going to listen. No one listens.

You're not really going to hear. No one hears.

You're not really going to care. No one cares.

But I will tell you my story anyway. I will tell you my story because you have asked to hear my story.

But that is all. You want my story from me: I do not want anything from you.

I do not want your pity.

I do not want your understanding.

I am giving you my story. You are giving me nothing.

When you have heard my story, you can tell others. You can tell the story any way you want to tell the story. I do not care. It does not matter. It does not mean anything.

Because no one listens.

And no one hears.

And no one cares.

I come from a village far away. We were farmers. That was our life. We had sheep and a shop. We had two cars. We had our religion. We are Kaka'i.

You do not know Kaka'i. It is our own religion. We are like the Yazidi. You gave the Nobel Prize to a Yazidi woman, but you know nothing about the Yazidi. We are like the Yazidi.

I can tell you about life in my village. But you do not care about life in my village. It was normal life. Normal life in the village.

ISIS came. They took my brothers. My father told me to run. So I ran.

I ran into Syria. I ran into Turkey. I ran and I walked and I travelled by bus and by car, into Bulgaria, into Serbia, into Hungary, and then into Norway.

You do not know what this is like. I can show you videos. But it makes no difference. You do not care. You will not hear. You will not listen.

I was in Norway. What is Norway? I did not know what Norway is. I had never seen another country. Norway is another world. In Norway there is a television programme, the title of the programme is *Where No One Would Believe That Someone Could Live*.

Norway is very cold. I have never known such cold. There are mountains and there are rivers. In Norway there are thousands of lakes and rivers and the waters are full of fish. I do not know the name of the fish. They are fish that live in the cold.

In Norway, the government puts us in an old army building. There are many of us in the building. It is not a good place. There is no hot water. We cannot wash. And we cannot work. At home, in my country, I was a farmer. Here, in Norway, in the cold, I am nothing.

I do not sleep at night. I have not heard from my family. I can never go home. I will never see anyone in my family again: my mother, my father, my sister, my brothers. They were killed by ISIS, or by the American bombs. How can I live like this? I will never be happy again.

In the daytime I would walk for one hour to the sea and go fishing. I do not know how to fish, but I fish. There is a fishing rod. I am wearing someone else's clothes. I have a pair of trousers and a jacket, a pair of shoes. I do not have my own clothes. I am standing by the water in Norway, in the cold, in someone else's clothes, with a fishing rod.

On the first day I caught two fish.

I did not eat the fish. I do not know the name of the fish. They are fish that live in the cold. I went back and said, who wants the fish, and they ate the fish with potatoes and spices.

Every day I go fishing in the cold. I do not like the fishing, but when I am fishing I think only about the fishing. I do not think about everything else.

One day I met a girl in the village, a Norwegian girl, at a concert, and we talked. We talked in English. But her father told her that she mustn't speak to me again.

The Norwegians did not want us.

No one wants us.

Nowhere wants us.

Nowhere listens.

Nowhere hears.

Nowhere cares.

From Norway I travel to Germany and then I travel to France, and then I travel here. The bus. The car. Under the truck. I can show you the videos.

I came here in a refrigerated truck. In France, I learn to stitch up the truck using my shoelace. It was dark. There is no air. I was so cold. It was much colder even than Norway.

I learned from the cold. In Norway, the fish grow larger in the cold. But the cold in my body, it is in my heart. I thought I was going to die. It would be better for me if I was dead. In the cold, I realise that life is nothing. I realise that life makes no sense, that bad things happen, and that no one listens and no hears and no one cares.

Now you have my story. And I still have nothing.

The Erased Person's Tale

as told to

Jonathan Wittenberg

'Earth, do not conceal my blood;
space, do not confine my cry' – *Job*

I LOOKED ONLINE AND immediately found the title of S's book. This was exactly as the judge who eventually granted him asylum had noted: anyone in his native country who wanted to check S's political record in order to persecute him had only to google his name. The book is a study of democracy and its failings in Africa. S has also published scholarly papers on the nature of language.

I meet S for the first time at the British Library, an institution devoted to the preservation of words, voices, testimony, knowledge. He tells me about his experiences of flight and refuge, focusing on what he saw and heard while held in indefinite detention here in Britain. 'You've no voice when you're inside there,' he says.

But S does have a voice. He has a degree in modern languages from the University of Strasbourg, a Master of Arts from the School for Oriental and African Studies (SOAS), and has taught for many years in London schools, with a special focus on inspiring children from ethnic minorities. It takes only a few moments in his company to understand that he has a gift for communicating gentleness, energy and enthusiasm. He is skilled at helping others to find their voice.

So, I ask him, why does he want me, or anyone else, to tell his story? Wouldn't it be more powerful coming directly from him? His response is that he needs someone else to hear, a person outside the immediate experience, to acknowledge and record what happened to him and to those whose sufferings he saw and shared. He wants me to be his witness, not because his narrative requires verification, but because of the fact of hearing itself; because it signifies that in a world which so often seeks to deny and disbelieve such accounts, his story has been absorbed by a listening heart.

We talk together for hours and, as I note down what he tells me, fearful of making mistakes, I become a partner in testament to the ongoing reality of cruelty and suffering. This is an obligation to which I am deeply committed; my own parents were both refugees from Nazism at the age of sixteen. Researching the fate of my family taught me the importance of being a vigilant witness against evil and heartlessness and to stand up for human solidarity, beyond all seeming borders of nationality and creed.

As I listen and record, I become a companion in defiance against the silence in which vicious regimes try to bury the knowledge of the crimes they have committed against the dead and disavow the living trauma of those who manage to survive them.

S needs me, us, to be allies.

★

He fled on foot with his family from the brutality of the regime in X___. During their long and exhausting trek which lasted for 30 days, he saw many people worn out from hunger, weariness and grief. Noticing an abandoned child who no longer had the strength to walk, S carried him on his back until he became aware that his body was lifeless.

After three months in exile, S and his family were told that it was safe to return to their homeland. They took the boat back across the river to their native country, but as the crowded ferry approached the landing beach, all the young men were separated out for questioning, to assess whether they might have been part of the militia fighting against 'government forces'. Anyone suspected of belonging to such rebel groups was removed and 'eliminated' without a trace. The militia in turn opened fire on the passengers, many of whom were killed. 'It was chaos; people took revenge, lots were shot,' S recalled. Four hundred people perished in the massacre.

S, his brother and their two cousins were taken away and detained for several days. He and his brother were subsequently released, but their cousins were never seen again. They simply 'disappeared', together with many hundreds of young people. 'He was with me on the boat. After we landed, I never saw him again.'

S began to work with the families of the victims, many of whom had likewise 'vanished'; no graves were ever found. Relatives were concerned that those responsible for the killings would never be brought to justice. A collective was formed to gather together the evidence of these atrocities; many of the survivors were afraid to come forward and testify, fearing that the regime would take revenge. Nevertheless, with the assistance of human rights organisations in Britain and France, enough material was assembled to force a trial at a criminal court in X___ in the summer of 2005. The judge ruled that the state was indeed responsible, but no specific individuals were deemed accountable and the perpetrators remained unnamed. The result was that no one was brought to justice.

During the course of their investigations, S and his colleagues uncovered numerous crimes. Realising that they knew too much to be safe in a land in which tyranny and corruption were incomparably more powerful than the law, he and his close family fled to France. There, life was better. S studied, obtaining his first degree in modern languages from the University of Strasbourg. Yet, perhaps inevitably, he always felt like an outsider. Later, S was invited to read for an MA at

SOAS, University of London, so moved his family to Britain and was eventually given a 'Tier Four' visa as a 'highly skilled migrant'.

S settled down in London, working for five years at a school in Islington, supporting children from ethnic minorities and assisting in the Modern Languages department. He also served as a volunteer in several homelessness projects through his church and began to assemble and publish his writings.

But it always remained his long-term intention 'to go back home and work for my country'. He was even offered a university post there, but it was made patently clear to him he was not wanted in X___, and that it would not be safe to return. When his father died, neither he nor any of his brothers and sisters were able to attend the funeral.

In 2015 S therefore decided to apply for asylum in Britain. He prepared the necessary documentation with great care, including the latest United Nations information concerning X___, a report commissioned from a Stanford University professor known internationally for his research on the country, a further dossier by an expert in the UK, and an eleven-page letter explaining his personal history and the circumstances underlying his application.

During his appointment with the Home Office, the official who interviewed him kept interrupting him. It quickly became apparent that she had read none of the documents S had submitted. Matters proceeded in this desultory fashion until, eventually, the woman instructed him to wait. After two hours she returned and informed S that he was going to be detained forthwith, 'for a few days, while the case is examined'.

This attitude epitomises the environment of intentional hostility, the culture of disbelief, which those at the top are held to be encouraging. There is a time and a place for scepticism. But the persistent discrediting of the meticulously assembled and carefully corroborated evidence of another person's suffering is a form of cruelty. It undermines the humanity both of the victims, and also of those who practice such policies.

S was taken to the detention centre at Harmondsworth. 'At first it looks beautiful,' he said, 'from the outside. There's no barbed wire. But once inside, you go through a first and then a second set of security doors. You're locked in; you can't open them from the inside. It's really a prison. There's nothing to do in there.' It was very frightening: 'There are some there too who've just completed sentences for serious crimes. When they're released, they're handed over to Immigration – together with people who're simply seeking asylum.'

S.'s smartphone was taken from him and replaced with a primitive device which allowed no access to the Internet. For the first two days he was simply bewildered. Then he began to contact his friends. Staff at the school where he worked soon started to ask where he was and what had happened to him. His church wondered why he was missing: 'Where is S?' they wanted to know; they were baffled and confused: 'No one could believe what had happened, that such a thing could occur here, in a country like Britain.' His friends had never even heard that such a place as Harmondsworth existed. They prepared an application for bail.

Injured physically and mentally by his own experiences, S was nevertheless more concerned with the sufferings of others: What about all the people who had no one on the outside to support them, who knew no one who could set in motion inquiries about why they had been taken away and where they were now being held? Who was there to help them?

> I saw a man sobbing. He told me he'd been in the UK for three years and held in detention for six months: 'When I was brought here my girlfriend was pregnant. Meanwhile she's given birth. I haven't ever seen our baby.'

Another man tried to kill himself twice during the two weeks I was being held. He did it out of despair. I heard he'd been inside for over a year. He didn't know when he was going to be released or how to move his case forward. He'd had no update. He didn't understand what it was that the authorities were waiting for. The first time, I don't know exactly what he did. They found him hanging from the bunk bed – he must have used the sheet or something similar and tied it round his neck. He was taken to hospital. A day later he was back. The second time, another guy from X___ was moved into his room. That man was on blood pressure medication; when he went out to get his food, he drank all his new companion's medicine. The toilets weren't private; you could see peoples' feet. Someone saw that he was in there for a long time. They opened the curtains. On the floor were all the pill packs, empty. They called the medical staff; they took him to hospital, for the second time in two weeks. They soon brought him back. He had no one outside to help him. I never heard that anyone had come to visit him.

S explained that the Home Office periodically required inmates to sign a standard letter agreeing to their continued detention on the basis that they couldn't be released because they had insufficient connections and support in London. The Home Office understood this as authorising them to keep the signatories in detention indefinitely.

I saw everyone in front of me sign. But they didn't understand the contents of the letter. 'Have you read it?' I asked one man. 'No; I can't read English'.

When my own turn came, I tried to read the letter first. 'Why can't you just sign?', the lady insisted. I went out for fifteen minutes and read the document. I came back and told her I wasn't signing. 'You have to', she said, 'It's just our routine.' 'No, I don't,' I replied. I'd been living in London for ten years; I refused to sign. I asked the lady what had happened to my file.

The administration isn't fit for purpose.

One man told me how he'd been in and out of detention for two years. For the last couple of months inside he'd heard nothing about his case. 'I'm going back to my home country,' he said. He'd had enough; he was giving up. They wear people down until they lose hope and agree to be deported.

S was allocated a duty solicitor and a different official was sent from the Home Office to interview him. He again gave his statement. The Home Office official explained that his application had been refused. 'They make a decision, then you have the right to appeal,' S explained. He prepared the appeal himself: 'If you can't write out your case for yourself, your solicitor can't do anything as he or she has at least 50 other people to deal with.'

Meanwhile S became ill; the removal centre was so dusty and dirty that he began to cough. 'They pay people a pound an hour to clean,' – less than a tenth of the London living wage. One day he coughed up blood. This really frightened him, so he reported to the doctor who came to Harmondsworth twice a week. He was taken to the infirmary, where he was kept in isolation, suspected of having tuberculosis. He had to wear a mask and was not allowed out. After three days he had still been given no medicine, not even paracetamol; he was simply left to sit all day in the sick bay, waiting. But conditions were better in there; he had a room with a toilet and a small TV. Eventually he was asked to do a spittle test, which came back inconclusive. A second, and finally a third test, proved negative.

Still, S had to attend his appeal hearing in a mask. When the judge asked him why he was wearing such an item, he explained that he was suspected of having TB.

The judge, who was perceptive and well-intentioned, observed that this was a 'very complicated case which couldn't be decided in a day'. S recalled: 'She looked at me and said: "I don't see any reason why this person is here. This complex case has been mismanaged. Go home and I'll write to you."' She promised to contact him within three months and ordered his immediate release. She added that a copy of his book would be required for his future hearing, as well as an expert report on his native country.

It took S two further days to secure his release. In the meantime, he was brought back to the medical centre: 'All that time nothing happened.' He called his solicitor, who merely said, 'Oh, are you still there?' The medical staff had no idea what was supposed to happen next.

Eventually S was taken to G4S who claimed that they had received no notification about him being released. He had no choice but to stay a further night in detention while he tried to trace for himself who it was who was supposed to be responsible for organising his release.

'I was there for just two weeks and it had an impact on my mental health. What about those who were in there for six months?'

The Home Office informed S that he was henceforth not allowed to work. Unable to earn any money for himself, S was dependent on his friends, who proved unstinting in their support. They made good on their offer to provide him accommodation for free. They looked after him with care and devotion; they raised the money to appoint him a good solicitor.

But the anticipated letter never arrived. 'They'd discovered their mistake,' S commented. Eventually the solicitor called, only to be informed that they had no record of him ever being in detention.

> They erased everything, to obliterate their error. That upset me more than anything else. I was the victim of a bureaucratic system where no one cares; where the decision is made beforehand and no one can be bothered.

After three months S was given a date to attend an appeal tribunal. Once again, he carefully prepared the latest and most updated reports about X___. He included letters of reference from his former employers at the school, from the priest of the church where he volunteered, as well as from a friend working at the Foreign Office. He included a copy of his book and his other writings, as the judge at Harmondsworth had advised. On the day itself, he came accompanied by his British girlfriend, his friend from the Foreign Office, and his priest, who brought his wife and his guide dog with him.

It proved to be 'a theatre of the absurd'. The court appointed an interpreter, even though S spoke and wrote excellent English and held two degrees in modern languages. The Home Office solicitor had neither read, nor even possessed copies of, any of the new documents. The judge deferred the proceedings for 30 minutes and provided her with the materials. She then proceeded to asked ridiculous questions, based on an outdated 2007 report, when S had provided the most recent 2015 findings. 'The Home Office hadn't even updated its information online,' S commented.

She asked S questions about his native country's rating, which should have been well-known to the Home Office; it ranked among the highest ever assigned for persecution, lawlessness and violence. She declared in conclusion that, 'Since a previous trial had been held, justice surely had no doubt been done.' S was left in tears.

The judge brought the proceedings to a close with the pronouncement that she was not going to make her decision on the spot. She would make it known within the following two weeks.

In her letter, which followed soon afterwards, she gave S leave to remain in the UK until 2020, noting that this had been granted on the basis of 'the evidence provided', with the added observations that 'one had only to type the referent's name into google to see that he would be arrested at once if he returned to his native country', and that, 'if he ever went back, even for a visit, he'd certainly have to change it.'

The tribunal determined that the case would be kept anonymous, purportedly on account of its sensitivity. 'But,' wondered S, 'was this the genuine reason? Or was it not rather that the Home Office was trying to cover up its confusion and erase the traces of the mess it had made?'

I asked S if he thought the system was cruel, callous, careless or just plain chaotic. 'The problem with the Home Office,' he said, 'is that you don't see the same person again. The next man or woman doesn't know your case; there's no real follow-up. The system is overloaded.' People themselves, he acknowledged, were as varied as anywhere else: some were unfeeling, some couldn't care, some were genuinely kind.

Had he pursued the reasons why his papers went missing? No, he indicated. He had started a new job in Whitechapel; he had become engaged and hoped to be married the following summer: 'My life has moved on since then.' Looking back was evidently too painful, and, at this juncture, pointless. It had taken six months to return to normal life.

But his experiences had left him with nightmares. 'And,' he said, 'I had friends on the outside to help me. Many of the people in there had nobody, not a soul to speak on their behalf.'

In the UK people don't disappear in massacres or acts of terror committed by the government or by militias whom everyone knows are implicated but no one has the power and authority to indict. That is why Britain and similar democracies are not places from which persecuted people generally long to escape. Their longstanding humanitarian tradition, their reputation for tolerance, and the widespread rule of law make them islands of refuge from state-sponsored murder and mass violence. People don't vanish into hidden mass graves.

But there are other ways of disappearing: when you've got no voice; when, even if you have, those around you don't, or won't, find the time to listen; when they lack the will to hear you in their conscience, or the compassion to care about you in their hearts.

You don't go missing, only your files do, and your presence in the thoughts of those who ought to care, and the record of the experiences which hurt you, and which drove others to despair.

The Observer's Tale

as told by

N

PURE DARKNESS.
Struggling to breathe in the cold refrigerated lorry.
Everyone says the air is finished.
So many different languages and everyone looking for a way to escape from death.
We welcome the police siren, which used to scare us all before.
But fatigue, weariness and the need for sleep don't give us the opportunity to celebrate the rescue from death.
A whisper of people in an unfamiliar language outside the lorry; I wish they would not stop opening the door.
Suddenly it does open. We are getting out. It is unclear whether our teeth are chattering with fear or cold.
Everything is dusky: mind, air, future, tomorrow.
Radio behind radio.
I do not know if my head is bowed for my sense of loss, my anxiety, my vague future.
I say to myself, 'Maybe sleep will make me better.'

We take the police car to the police station.
Their sweet biscuits don't take away the bitterness of the story.
We are ordered out of our clothes and are checked.

I am questioned from head to foot.
I have neither the energy nor the language to ask anything back.

Desperately, I say to myself, 'Let the wind carry me wherever it wants.'

Through the interpreter, they ask hundreds of questions of a man drowned in thoughts and sorrows.

Space is fierce. You do not hear anything other than the sound of iron: key chains, handcuffs, steel bars.

God, why am I so far away from my grandfather's orchard? Not the sound of water, not the nightingale, nor the spring. What if I am guilty? What will happen? I have no answer except, 'Endure – you live with hope.'

Finally, everyone is pushed into a dark and dirty room with a toilet next to the bed. I think the human rights charter is written for us upside down!

The peephole is raised. He asks, 'Tea or coffee?' I say 'Tea' – without the magic word.

The style of hospitality is different here. No one can eat their tasteless food.

Alone in a rough room, my eyes rent the liquid from my mouth. It hurts me that I do not know how long I am staying in this room, but I know I cannot be friends with this brutal cage.

The door opens. My filthy clothes, messed up hair, overgrown beard, all induce a sense of being accused. I am different so I am accused.

They want to take me to another place. Get back to the van for a long journey. The tattoos of the officers are anonymous and scary, to be honest. I hope they have mixed me up with someone else.

Here is Dover. Inside the immigration office there are the sounds of scratching paper sheets, the click click of a camera,

the tick tick of officers' walking.
No one talks.

I am hearing my name. I will follow the sound's source.
I sit on the chair opposite the officer.
I cannot keep my head up as my appearance is like my lamentable mental state.
Question behind the question: 'Who are you? How did you come here? Why did you come? Blah, blah, blah.'
I say to myself, 'I wish he would stop soon.'
I can't think straight.
Whatever comes to you.
The man is asking me, 'Why do you not like detention?'
I say to the interpreter, 'Because no one likes it.'
Synchronously I tell myself, 'As though I have a choice!'

I see other people there who are disturbed and distracted.
They take me back to the tattoos, to another unfamiliar place.
I do not know why these people hold me tight. I didn't sleep for a few nights and did not eat any food. I don't even have the energy to walk!
I am dragged inside.
I don't know where I am but certainly it is not like a hotel.
Now it is midnight in Reception.

I am trying to ask, 'Where is here?' But my English is not enough.
There are many other people of other nationalities.
Through their faces I can say, 'Here is not a good place.'

They call me out.
Someone is taking me to an allocated room.
I have never seen someone hold so many keys at one time.
I am following him passively.
With the opening of each iron door, my hope of return is getting less and less, as if the whole, heavy weight of these doors

is on my shoulders.

As the count of doors goes up, I think about my grandmother saying, 'Hell is seven floors.'

Even if they say, 'Get out!' I can't.

The way of my coming was a maze, like the way of my future.

It is morning.

I am opening my eyes.

I see a small window with large bars facing out on to another wing.

What is the meaning of a window, I wonder, that you cannot open?

This window is like my problem. There is no way out.

I don't know when I fell asleep.

I am singing gently in my language:

'This is the beginning of the cold season.

A pain is always found behind my beliefs.'

Inja aghaze fasle samast, hamishe dardi poshte arezuhayam peydast

Officers open the doors for the rooms for breakfast.

I am looking at other detainees to know what to do.

Everyone has a plastic container in their hand.

Downstairs, down the staircase.

People with different shapes and nationalities, but the dishes are all the same colour.

Some are walking loose along the wing, as if eating takes their energy.

I have lots of questions to ask, but since I have not yet accepted that I should stay here I will not ask.

At the breakfast table I recognise something in the appearance of those who speak my language. I don't know why I don't like to say anything. I am looking at two people who whisper with

each other and then they turn to me.
They chat with me. They show me the way of life here beneath the surface.
They say –
Nobody knows when they will be released.
No rule.
Not predictable.
Everything is by chance.
They are likely to send you back.
This is a removal centre (such a soft word).

They carry on –
'You need to be careful about drug dealers.'
In the meantime someone who wears low-slung trousers passes.
After he has passed they say –
'He is one of them.'

They continue to talk and I am curious to know why whatever they are saying is negative.
What is happening to me?
Then they say –
'This place has gangs. You have to be very careful.'

I don't want to hear any of this, despite my curiosity, and I would like to change the topic but I can't think of anything to say.
I have never known myself so impotent and insignificant.
It's been a long time since I have seen myself in a mirror.
At the same time I miss and hate myself.

The first days of my life here were spent trying to find a reason for being detained.
I didn't have a motive for going to the bathroom. Even if I had, I had no clothes to change into.
They just gave me a set of black undergarments. Just wearing these degrading clothes, my sense of helplessness was greater.
Now it is around a week that I have been detained.

Somebody is looking for me with a file, as today the caseworker talked with me.
Perhaps I am being released.
Somebody is translating his words –
'This place was just temporary, now we are going to move you to the permanent wing.'

It is bitter news.
I say to myself –
'Every day is worse than the one before.'

I put my stuff in a rubbish bag and follow officers.
After a complicated path, a small door opens into a huge space with three floors instead of two.
More crowded.
People call it The Gangster Capital.

Actually some people here are living well. They have everything: business, drink, computer games. Perhaps not wives and girlfriends. They even seem to be making money.
Everything is a mystery.

When I get in, some look at me.
Unwillingly, with head down and without words, I go to a filthy room.
Just a bed without a sheet, a table and TV.
Here is where I have to live, for an indefinite time.

When I look through the window into the opposite wing I think I have to be strong and not give up.

I list the things my room needs. I go to the IT room to translate the words to English. I make my room a lot better.
I am talking more with people in my own languages.
I am trying to be positive – pray, meditate, talk.
Sometimes I am well.

Sometimes it doesn't work.

At certain times, and only then, you are free to leave the wing and get out into the communal places. I have to plan for that.

I am going to the canteen.
Here there is a long queue but my card still has enough money to buy food.
They give us 70p each day.

Between 10 and 12 o'clock is an important time for detainees, as people will be released at this time.
All of us, in our heads, approach the Home Office door at this time.
Some come back happy, most with sadness.
The single most used sentence at this time is, 'Are you released?'

Each day I stay I see injustice and cruelty.
Some people use drugs.
Some earn money.
Some are beaten.
Some people turn a blind eye.
In short, everything here is based on luck.

So I must try to think positively – pray, meditate, talk.
Read a book, practice English and anything that can help me.

I say to myself, 'In this place, you don't have anyone to help you, talk to you, and so on.'
Anyhow, just being positive at this moment can help me.
But when whatever I see is negative, I don't know how.

9am, after breakfast, the door of the wing is opened and I go to English classes.
Every morning I see one man who doesn't eat for a long time; doesn't take a shower; doesn't talk to anyone.

He gets weaker every day. His mustard brown jacket is becoming wider every day.

The coloured posters in the English classes take me away momentarily from a monotonous world.

I compare myself to one of the posters with the caption, 'She is laughing'. It takes me on an imaginary journey.

In the corridors on the way back, the smell of smoke and sweat and spice is nauseating.

Later I see the man in the mustard brown jacket.

I can't see his eyes.

His head is bowed.

I want to pretend that here is normal but every time I see that man I feel sick.

An intense clash in the wing is taking place among the detainees.

A lot of blood is shed.

The male guards do not intervene but the female officers resolve the issue.

This happens a lot here, but it never changes the speed of the step of the man in the mustard brown jacket.

Nothing can attract his attention.

I would like to talk to him but he does not even notice me.

I don't have enough money to buy food like the other men.

Also, I can't sleep at night so I make a decision to work for detention.

The irony isn't lost on me.

Each night, £4.

I can buy an energy drink and a peanut bar for my friend and me to eat in the yard, as we sit and look at the sky and the tops of trees.

To be honest, when I see birds fly more freely I can't feel life is normal any more.

While I am tracking the bird's flight I feel as if I am choking.

I am doing my best to be positive.
I am trying to give positive energy to anyone who has just come into detention.
I don't ask anybody about their Home Office decision as I know mostly they are hopeless.

I talk to people more.
I play some games.
I want to laugh.
I want to laugh at my fate.

At 2 o'clock in the morning the letters are thrown into the rooms.
Unconsciously I wake up at this sound.
I am hopeful I will be released soon, but this morning's letter is for my roommate.
Several times I have seen a roommate released.
To be honest I will miss this one, if he is.

I can't sleep.
I am thinking about my family, my friends in my country, my mother's food.
Why does the Home Office keep me here?
Surely it's obvious my own sadness is enough.

I am angry that I can't be positive.
Sobs stick and tighten in my throat when I think that the small opening of the peephole is the most I can wish for.
The feeling of disability and humiliation turns the calm of sleep into hate and anger.
Of course, it is unfair on me that my tears must be concealed behind a heavy metal door.

The next day my roommate is released. This is the fourth time.
Goodbyes, when someone is released, are agonising.
Everyone is gathered in the IT room around the freed person.

He goes and I get back to my room, looking at the silly T-shirt he left behind.
I remember his sadness, his words, his jokes.
And most of all his joy after freedom.
I remember once I asked him, 'If you were a bird where would you go?'
And he said, 'I would come to this place and I would shit on it.'

This place is like a caravanserai, but no one knows how long some of us will stay behind.

After months, the decision is made to send me back.
When all the detainees are sleeping the guards come to me and say, 'In a quarter of an hour we will come back to remove you.'

With general misfortune I resist. I refuse to be sent back.
I am sent to the solitary block immediately for refusing.

After some days I am released from a state of specific, localised detention to a more generalised one, full of lovely, generous, friendly people, but where work, rebuilding my life and travelling abroad are banned, where waiting is my evening meal, and my guest when I fall asleep is a nightmare of bars and cells.

The Listener's Tale

as told to

Gillian Slovo

OF THE CAPACITIES LIFE has gifted me, a sense of direction is not included. And Jane, as it turns out, shares this problem. She can be so clueless about geography, she tells me, that when her friends heard that she was going to be a Refugee Tales walk leader they warned her that she was going to get the whole group hopelessly lost. 'I'll do a dummy run,' she laughingly reassures me. 'It will be okay.'

I look at her as she sits across from me in my living room. She is so contained, so quietly spoken and also so quietly confident (and I think – but this I keep to myself – so *English*) that I, who am also accustomed to continually getting lost, believe her.

I ask her about her early life. She tells me that she was born in England, lived for a time in the US, and then after coming back and travelling round for a while, she ended up in a different country (not named to preserve anonymity) with her mother. The experience gave her a taste of what it is like to find yourself a stranger in the midst of others. 'It sounds, ridiculous,' she says, 'but growing up in that country with an English mum who was divorced, possibly the only divorced mother in the city, where there was real hatred against the English. Real hatred,' she repeats, 'so I certainly had a flavour of not being welcome.'

Aha, I thought, hearing in this a double clue. Not only the roots of her understanding of what it feels like to be discriminated against because of the accident of your birth, but also, the way that crossing oceans and geographical divides messes with a person's sense of direction.

I ask her more about herself.

A former solicitor whose husband's work often takes him away from home, she spent some years as a stay-at-home mother to their four children. When her kids were older she was looking around for volunteer work and she happened upon an advert for a local visitor's group. 'I had no idea about the charity,' she said, 'or the fact that we detained people. It had never crossed my mind before – it was screaming out, and I had no idea.'

Her voice is calm as she says this, as it remains throughout all of our conversations. I first met her when she picked me up to drive me to a detention centre that was near to where she lived. Contrary to my every preconception, the detainee I met there was happy: an Italian who had been in prison, he was awaiting deportation and, he told me, counting the days until he could be reunited with his home and his family. An unexpected encounter since he had a home to go to and a family with the resources to welcome him back. Not so, I assumed, for the only other detainee in that large, soulless room. As the Italian leaned forward to tell us how delighted he was to be finally quitting Britain, a woman opposite the other man kept up a steady stream of conversation. Despite the woman's bright enthusiasm, the man just sat there. I watched him out of the corner of my eye: I was trying to work out whether he was interested in what she was saying or whether he even understood her. He stayed very still, as if the words she was throwing his way had nothing to do with him, and then she must have said something out of kilter because he leaned forward in his chair to shout: 'No. It is not like that.' Perhaps the woman opposite him flinched or perhaps he registered how loud his voice had been. He opened his hands, palms up, in a gesture of apology before sinking back into his previous lethargy.

Jane is a veteran of such moments. She has so far visited 25 detainees, some of them for as long as a year, and she can still remember all their names and tell me about each one of them. I ask her how she copes being witness to so much pain and she answers, as openly and honestly as she answers everything: 'I just feel that the purpose of being there,' she says, 'is to support people in detention and the only way I can help is to listen. I can't change anything but I can hold hands, and I can listen, and not always to their life stories. Sometimes we just talk about football, or what's on television, or the weather, anything just to make a good hour for them so they don't fall into that hole of desperation.'

But what, I asked, if like the man I observed in the detention centre, they are already deep down in that hole? If your mission is to listen, what happens if the other person won't say anything? This is the only moment in our long conversation when Jane looks anything other than cheerful. She drops her voice to tell me the story of one man she visited who, for the whole first month, just sat with his head down. In the beginning, she said, she tried to make small talk, but then she realised that this was ridiculous and so, instead she also sat unspeaking. At the end of an hour, she would tell him that she had to go and he would say: 'Thank you ma'am, thank you for coming,' and then, when she asked if he wanted her to come back, he would say yes. After a while, she said, he did begin to talk, always with his head down, and what he talked about were the terrible sequence of events that had forced him from his home. He was an Indian, she told me, who was really tall, over six foot, but he always seemed tiny. She listened to what he had to say, hoping that her listening would make him feel less alone, but in the end she had to stop seeing him, not because he was deported or let out of there, but because he said her visits weren't helping. She immediately started visiting somebody else, it was the best thing she could do to get over this defeat, but on her weekly forays to the detention centre she would always ask the people at the desk to check if that man was still around. He was for a while, until one day when he wasn't. She doesn't know what happened to him: he had been swallowed up by geography to who knows where. 'I have to let it go,' she tells me: 'but I will remember forever and I will know what happened. Even if it's only me remembering, that's the only thing that's going to last. Because nobody cares about him.' She sits, quietly, for a moment and I see her sadness that, for this almost stranger, her listening was not sufficient as she says: 'I wonder if anybody knows if he's still alive.'

But there are others, she says as she brightens, who have stayed in her life. Some who have been deported but who continue to message her from around the globe, and some who are in the UK, still jumping through the endless asylum hoops. On their release from detention, already driven by circumstance from one part of the globe to the other, they become the victims of a different kind of geographical shift. Forbidden from working, they are placed in Section 4 accommodation in unfamiliar parts of the country and told to report, sometimes weekly, to a designated police station. Their housing is paid for and they are given an Azure Card that is meant to cover their weekly food budget – to be purchased only from certain shops. But an Azure Card can't be used on public transport. As a result some of them have a weekly twenty mile trek to the police station and back – if, that is, they actually make it back.

Jane tells me about one such man who, as he is on the way to report, thinks about strangers and the position of police station doors: experience has taught him that if there is an unfamiliar man loitering at the police station desk or if there is a door open to one side, then these are the warning signs that he is about to be re-detained.

'They will just take him through the door,' she tells me, 'and say, you're coming this way, no explanation given.'

One man she's in touch with who is in Newport and who is now required to sign every two weeks, lives a relatively happy life. But in the two days before he is due to report he goes inside himself, becoming a recluse in fearful anticipation of a possible re-detention. He has reasons for this fear: it has so far happened to him on three separate occasions. On one of these, he was taken through the open door to be driven by van from the police station in Newport to a detention centre in Dorset. It shouldn't have happened since his case was still pending (detention is supposed to be for those about to be deported) but still it took his solicitor three weeks to get him released at which point he was put in a taxi, courtesy of the state, and driven all the way back to Newport. Another of the people that Jane still keeps in touch with was sent to live in Section 4 housing in Sheffield. When he was re-detained, he was held for so long that by the time he was released his housing had been given to someone else. So, he was dispatched to Coventry where he stayed only to be later re-detained, after which he was sent, on release, to live in Birmingham.

Welcome to Britain and the manner in which people, who can't even afford to take a bus, get to see the country.

Jane brings up geography again when I ask her whether her friends are resistant to the work she does with detainees. Some are, she tells me and then she tells me about one of them, a friend, a neighbour, who thinks that seeking asylum in this country is wrong but who had himself worked in India for a year. 'He got a good job,' she tells me, 'and came home on holidays yet he can't see the similarities between himself and those I listen to in detention. 'What would you do?' she asks me as she has asked him, 'If you were providing for your family and you couldn't make any money, what would you do? You'd go somewhere where the jobs were. That's what any of us would do.' And, she went on, the Home Office was continually breaching its own rules. 'In a UK context the way the authorities behave has surprised me,' she continues. 'I thought better of us and of government organisations. I thought we didn't break rules. Now I know that's not the case.'

Her anger at this is almost immediately muted by her telling me why she keeps on with her listening life. It helped her, she said, when her mother was ill and when both her sons were facing difficulties. Then it was good to spend an hour when she didn't think about her problems because she was with people whose life challenges were so much more acute than hers. 'In today's world,' she says, 'and even in my little world, to sit without a mobile phone or anything else, to sit for an hour or so with somebody else and you're not trying to achieve something, it's really unusual. And it's actually really powerful for that... because it calms you down. It makes you stop, it makes you take stock of what's going on the world, the bigger world, the smaller world, what's actually important to people. To see people in detention as human beings, wherever they're from, and to hear about real problems. I think it's a good thing to sit and listen. Even the silences which I don't like....' She pauses before continuing: 'There are a lot of people I'd like to make do this. And even though people will tell me terrible things,' and now she has truly brightened up, 'they will also tell me something wonderful: How the mountains look where they used to live, how the stream comes down. I've got a lot out of it,' she says. 'I've got a sense that I'm befriending people in detention, a sense that I'm helping build pressure on how to change the system and meeting fantastic people, not just in detention.'

And of course, it won't surprise you, that she ended thus: 'while also learning more about geography.'

The Teacher's Tale

as told to
Emma Parsons

YOUR CARD FOR X arrived safely. Thanks. I saw him this morning. I was hoping this email would describe a happy day with him. But no. He's now frightened and lonely and back in a detention centre costing the taxpayer as much as it cost us to keep mum in the care home.

★

It was 7 November. Cold. A Monday. The plan was for me to meet you at the Home Office reporting centre near London Bridge and then have a coffee in the Southwark Cathedral cafe, followed by a walk along the river. But because you had nothing pending in the system – because you were between losing your appeal and lodging a fresh claim for asylum, and because you had received a letter from the Home Office saying that they planned to deport you and your embassy was in the process of preparing travel documents – I feared that the coffee and walk might not happen. It's why I suggested we met there in the first place. I didn't know the system; I was worried they might take you straight to the airport. With no money.

★

He was happy when he met me at the reporting centre this morning. He had cut his own hair so was wearing a baseball cap because he said he couldn't reach the back bits properly and his head was cold; he had heard that he could finally register with a doctor and he was looking forward to spending the rest of the morning with me. I met him at 10am, before he reported. We queued up together. He finally went in at 10.30am. I was told to wait outside. In the cold. Fifteen minutes later, he came out looking anxious to tell me that he had been told he had to see his caseworker. Bad sign. I waited for two hours. I kept trying to wait inside the building because it was freezing, but each time I went in, the security guards told me to go back and wait outside. Finally, an official came with a message from him saying to go home because he had not been seen yet, so I told the official to tell him I would be five minutes away in a café. I went to the Southwark Cathedral café which is very peaceful and quiet – and waited. An hour later he phoned. Not on his phone. They wouldn't let him use that. He had been told that they were going to detain him pending getting travel papers for deportation, but at that point he didn't know where they were going to send him. Maybe back to Harmondsworth, he didn't know. I could tell he was trying not to cry. It was awful. I left messages on his solicitor's voicemail and stormed back to the reporting office and pleaded with one of the guards to find out if I could at least get his keys so that I could go and get his belongings and take them to him later in the detention centre. I waited. And waited. Waiting is a synonym for the whole bloody system. His keys were finally handed over, but I wasn't allowed to see him.

★

I went to Walthamstow to get your things. The place was empty. The grumpy roommate who never talks to you was out. I let myself in. Your little corner of the room was just as you had left it that morning (it reminded me of entering my brother's room after his sudden death). Your bed was unmade; lines of socks and underpants draped over the headboard and a T-shirt drying over the back of your only chair – the green T-shirt that had been too small for my son. On the floor, neatly lined up: a *cafetière* full of green tea; a jar containing your toothpaste, your shaving cream; two huge bags of rice; several brochures from adult education colleges; your bible; dictionaries; the little souvenir turtle from Turkey; and piles and piles of papers: Home Office documents annotated in black by you and red by me; verb lists, exercises, library opening times; plastic bags full of tubes of watercolour paints and brushes... I was embarrassed to intrude on this, your only private space, but who else was going to get your things?

★

And so it's back to the acronyms, tiresome words and chairs that produce backache. This is the new routine. Every Tuesday evening after school, cycle to London Bridge and catch the train south. There is an hourly shuttle bus to the detention centre, but it's easier to walk. I pass the lines of families checking in for holidays and exit the terminal past the small WHSmith and the toilets at the rear. This is the exit to back stage of the airport. I pass cabin crew, airport officials and cleaners on the stairs that lead down to the perimeter road. It is a 35-minute walk alongside the runway. Desolate. Dark. Not designed for pleasure. The verges are narrow and dirty (no sign of rubbish collection here); the passing cars are close. This is mesh and barbed wire country – warehouses, prefab offices, Hangar 6, and car parks where only the correctly programmed lanyard will activate the barriers' access control systems. And then there are the planes; the strangeness of seeing the huge fuselage of a stationary airbus 380, empty of passengers; the air-shimmer and smell of jet fuel as planes take off and land. On Tuesday evenings in winter Perimeter Road South is empty of people.

★

The visiting hours are 2pm-9pm. I will only have about an hour with you. There is an advance booking system, but I still have to wait. It's not called a detention centre; it's called an IRC, an Immigration Removal Centre. It's run by a private security firm. I remember reading about a security firm escorting Jimmy Mubenga to his death by suffocation on a plane deporting him to Uganda. Jimmy Mubenga was a deportee. You are not yet a deportee. You are still a detainee. Anonymising appellations. Neat. One word.

Apart from its high mesh fence, locked security gates and row of small windows on the second storey overlooking the runway, the IRC could be the HQ of a prosperous little company on the outskirts of town – landscaped shrubs, a clean paved path leading up to a pillared portico with polished glass doors. Next to the Reception is a metal walk-through security arch.

I know the procedure. I show my passport. I empty my pockets. I put my bag and coat in a locker. I am issued with a wristband. I hand over the cards of hope and support from my family, a mobile phone voucher, a set of drawing pencils (a present from the art coordinator at school) and the books you have asked for – I am not allowed to give these things to you directly. You will be given a receipt which you will use to collect them later. I go through the curtain at the back, stick my arms out and a female guard politely pats me down (one last check) before I go through the metal security arch (one more last check) and am taken into the visitors' room. Then I wait. I have nothing to read, so I look around the room. Large. Low ceilinged. A vending machine in one corner. A pile of toys in another, near a high-mounted telly. One guard by the exit, another at the back by the door through which you will come.

★

Your computer is at my house. You're not allowed it. You're not allowed your phone either. They've given you one without a camera, without Internet access. You want to carry on where you left off with the adult literacy lessons at Waltham Forest

College. A good English language course would have been better but there wasn't one. Now all we have time for is another kind of English altogether, not Adult Literacy, not ESOL (English for Speakers of Other Languages) not EFL (English as a Foreign Language), not EAL (English as an Additional Language): the English we are forced to work on is EDL (English as a Detention Language) and it's no fun. Instead of role-plays – going shopping, in a café, at the doctor's – we are hunched over the esoteric words and exhausting syntax that will determine your life.

★

In the visitor's room, we are not allowed to sit side by side, so we sit opposite each other and have to angle our bodies so we can both see the latest letter from your solicitor or the Home Office. It's not just the words (appellant; respondent; alleges, purports; opportunistic; not credible – 'It means they don't believe you'), it's the whole structure. A thicket of dashes, dots, colons, colon-dashes, brackets (open and square), initials, acronyms, abbreviations, and numbers – reference numbers, clause numbers, sub-clause numbers, legal article numbers. And how to prioritise understanding?

> 2.18 Caselaw JC (double-jeopardy: Art 10CL) CG [2008] UKIAT 00036. See JC v Secretary of the State for the Home Department [2009] EWCA Civ 81

Helpful to understand at some point maybe, but this is more important right now:

> Submission 5. C ('C – Claimant. That's you') contends ('claims, says') that on at least one legitimate view of the facts ('I'm not quite sure what that means') the following propositions ('these are the things you propose, the reasons you give for claiming asylum')

could be made good and as such the claim is not clearly unfounded

'OK. Clearly unfounded. That is what the Home Office say. They say your fresh claim for asylum is no good. They say you don't give any good new reasons for claiming asylum and there's no evidence to back up –'

'Back up?'

'You have no proof. No evidence –'

'But I have evidence –'

'Exactly. Your solicitor is saying here that you do have evidence. This means your claim is not clearly unfounded. The following propositions – these ones here – 5A. 5B. 5C. – show that you are at risk if they send you back.'

I wish we were practicing the meaning of beautiful words.

★

He was very depressed this evening. He said he wasn't sleeping properly. He was getting sudden painful headaches and his heart was over-beating and keeping him awake. He said he couldn't concentrate. He said he hadn't collected the small, ceramic polar bear I brought him from Canada because he was worried someone might take it from his room.

★

You rarely talk about what happened to you. The reason you claimed asylum in the first place. But sometimes we have to talk about it – talk about what was at the heart of your original claim for asylum that was rejected.

We are working on the language in a doctor's report that will support your fresh claim for asylum. Unlike the Home Office, this doctor originally thought you were 'credible' and still does. But her report makes you tearful – not because the words are hostile and intimidating but because they are on your side and trigger something you don't want to remember. You have no problem with the meaning of the word torture. It's the other words I have to explain: flashback; deterioration of mental health; isolation; anxiety; post-traumatic stress disorder.

★

It's a race against time now. The fresh claim still hasn't been lodged and he's just received a letter headed Removal Directions. He's due to be deported in six days. A flight has been booked.

★

More words on your side. Pages and pages of them. We are looking at the final statements of support that will accompany your fresh claim for asylum. I am happy to go over these words: integrity, modest, dignified. You have made an impression on so many people since this ordeal began.

★

His fresh claim was rejected. I can't believe it. He was remarkably stoical about it. But the good news is that the solicitor managed to get the deportation order revoked. We are going to try and get him out on bail again. He's been in detention for six months now. It's worth a try. He talked a lot about God today. He knows it's not my thing, but I envy him it. It clearly helps him so much. He talked about retaining the freedom he feels inside. He said 'I have freedom in my heart. Because God lives, I can face tomorrow.'

The Applicant's Tale

as told by

F

It has been over two and a half years since my solicitor's letter said:

'This brings to an end the current immigration matter. As advised, you need to take steps several months prior to the expiry of your leave on 09.11.2018 to apply for further leave to remain. As you are on a 10-year route to settlement you will need to make three applications for further leave prior to being eligible for 'Indefinite Leave to Remain'. Each successive grant of leave will be for 30 months.'

Each application requires me to pay £3,000. This charge was increased just after I applied.

It had only taken nine and a half years for the Home Office to finally decide that I could work and they would grant me Discretionary Leave to Remain. During that time, I lived where they chose. For the first seven and a half years, I lived in five different properties in London. I lived with people who I did not choose to be with. I lived on the £35 a week they gave me. Then they moved me to St Leonards-on-Sea in East Sussex, they said because of a shortage of housing in London. I did not know anyone in East Sussex. I was arbitrarily 'shot' down to Hastings as fast as the legendary arrow that may have done for Harold.

After reading my solicitor's letter, I went to the nearest Citizens Advice Bureau. I felt a bit happy and said to the lady:

'It feels like I am just out of prison.'

She glanced at me and continued to fill in the form. Towards the end of the form she asked: 'What was the crime that you committed?'

I said, 'Pardon?'

'You said you were in prison, what was your crime?'

I laughed involuntarily.

Soon after this interview I became homeless as I had to leave the NASS (National Asylum Support Service) accommodation I'd been provided with, as my situation had changed. The Home Office decision meant I was now on my own trying to find somewhere to live and work.

The next stage was to attend the nearest Job Centre. I went for a couple of interviews, which reminded me of Yarl's Wood with all the security people around you, taking you downstairs, along corridors, and back up again. At one of my interviews the man asked me a couple of questions, all the time looking at the computer screen. The interview did not take very long. A couple of weeks later, I went back to the Job Centre and they said: 'You failed the Habitual Residency Test. You did not have any evidence to prove that you were living in the UK for the last nine and a half years.'

I felt like I was losing my mind and my self. I just started to shout in the middle of the job centre. That was the moment I realised why they had security people in job centres. First, they play their Byzantine games, then when you inevitably react to it, the guards step up to pacify you. Of course, I had papers from NASS but I had never been asked for them, it was all part of a system designed to wrong-foot you.

When I was made homeless, I sent emails to everyone I knew, entitled 'Help!' Most did not respond, some said, 'I am sorry and good luck.' These were not the words that I liked to hear. They were reminders of what I had heard most from people during the last nine and a half years. But, a very friendly person called Jean from Lewes heard my voice. We had met a year earlier on a Refugee Tales walk. She said that there was a couple who were offering their guest room for four weeks, which I happily accepted. Meanwhile I was working hard every day, sending CVs and writing covering letters. I sent my CV to over 40 places but had only three interviews. The last interview was for a full-time receptionist job in the oldest hotel in the heart of Lewes. I worked there for a year and saved enough money to enable me to apply for a bursary to go to university to study archaeology. With the help of the Lewes Organisation in Support of Refugees and Asylum Seekers (LOSRAS), a member offered me a low rent accommodation in her home, where I had a clean and peaceful room with my own bathroom. At last I had a place of safety and a support network.

I was lost and needed encouragement and so being taken to Lewes College by Valerie was hugely important. She urged me to register on a GCSE English class for three hours a week. I found volunteer work in an Archaeological Library where I catalogued books into their new software. During that summer I also worked on an archaeological excavation on my days off. I had to fill every hour I had and couldn't allow myself a spare moment to think about anything other than my goal: going to university. I'd already applied for a bursary the previous year and been refused because I had no money in an account and nobody to sponsor me, but I wouldn't give up.

I could cope like this, so long as no one poked me with their curiosity. Other people didn't understand: I was not a whole person, more like a set of glued-together fragments; a shattered piece of glass or Chinese porcelain held together with cement. Their questions threatened to shatter me all over again. And when they asked, everything leaked out of me, leaving me exhausted. It took weeks, sometimes months for me to forget what I'd been asked and get back to being able to sleep again, normally, without the nightmares. I was suffering the long-term effects of the endless court appearances, the refusals, the uncertainty, the nine and a half years of a hostile environment, the ceaseless questioning, the disbelieving, the constant reliving of a painful past.

F

What I did manage to do during this year in the peace and quiet of my room was to start telling 'my tale'.

★

'What Goes Around…'

After my experience in detention centres as an asylum seeker, I expected my circumstances to improve when NASS had to provide me with accommodation run by Clearsprings.

This is how I lived for five years: Bend down, mind your head, take five steps down into a cellar – this was my room. A window which couldn't be opened fully looks out on an overgrown garden, full of rubbish. A wardrobe made out of bits of wood and cardboard. The only friend I had was Rebecca, my name for a mouse that used to come out when the nightlight was on and things were quiet.

My fellow inmates in this place were all women. Some had babies. There were six rooms: three singles, three twins. Those that didn't have babies had to share with a stranger. One tiny, shared kitchen which was occupied by an army of cockroaches and more mice. How many times we called the man from Clearsprings to report the mice and cockroaches. Endlessly we called but nothing change. Sometimes men came into our rooms with no warning to check – we never had any idea what they were looking for.

How desperate I was to have my radiator working during the cold winter in London. We were not even allowed to have a small heater in our room. I hated every bit of that house where I had to live for five years.

Time passed. Almost five years later, I saw this housing officer from Clearsprings at my reception counter in Lewes, where I greeted people with a big smile and gave them information and made them comfortable while they are with us! He came… we both stood speechless. I had this unpleasant feeling. I felt colourful chemicals running all over my brain. I had a sudden flashback. I felt ashamed to remember living in that Clearsprings house. And now to be face-to-face with my prison officer

.

I tried my best to pull myself together – I was the hotel receptionist after all. I mumbled: 'Oh, I know you… from Wood Green.' As if I could ever forget him.

'Oh yes,' he said.

Before I had a chance to think, I said, 'If I knew it was you, I would have put you in a bad room…'

Then he said, 'Aah… I never liked working for Clearsprings,' and asked me what had happened to me. I quickly reassured him I was not working illegally. I proudly added that I had been granted my status, after nine years of struggle, and I would be going to university in the autumn. I asked him if he was going to dine in the restaurant; he thought a second and said no. I thought he would say that.

I was on the late shift that night. It had been the hottest day in England since 1975 and we didn't have air conditioning in the hotel. He called reception and asked if we had a fan he could use. I told him that we didn't.

★

I realise now I that I have benefitted from lots of people's helping hands; Jean was the first, then more joined to help. It was almost like Lord of the Rings. Wherever I wanted to be, a hand reached out to help me. Jean was joined by Arnold and Valerie, then Jane and Pat, then Alison and Betty, my landlady in Lewes. Some gave me accommodation to start me off; Alison sent me a bag full of vegan stuff. Valerie took me to Lewes College and cooked a vegan meal every day I stayed with her. Pat became my teacher and still edits my writings and essays. Jane visits me now I am in Winchester in my second year.

I am still moving around. This is my third house in this city in one and a half years. It is a most difficult thing to find a room for £100 a month! I had always wanted to study archaeology and after living for so long in pain I decided to study something that would please me rather than just bring me money. My classmates are half my age and they mostly look at me no doubt wondering why I am there in their class. Luckily there is someone in my class who is 65. I feel a bit relieved.

For the first time last week, I found myself jumping with happiness. The results came back for an assignment. I was not expecting a good grade and had to re-read my lecturer's comments many times, as he had awarded me a grade of 61%. This was the first time I had felt this happy in as long as I could remember; I was not used to being satisfied with results; I hadn't been with any over the previous ten years.

My immigration appeal results had always been profoundly depressing, and when I learned that I couldn't have access to a student loan with discretionary leave, my life felt empty all over again. Even when I sat down for my first university lecture, having finally got a bursary to study, I wasn't happy. Somehow I didn't believe it was real. I always felt like it was going to be taken away.

The Social Worker's Tale

as told to

Bernardine Evaristo

I WAS BORN INTO an era of military coups and wars and the imprisonment of all opponents of the government

I was born into a country where the new government persecuted my businessman father for his connections to a previous one

I was born into the wrong tribe at the wrong time in history

I was sent to school in the countryside for safety until war broke out there too – between the rebels of the North and government forces from the South

I had to escape school on foot with a suitcase on my head, fearful of passing through enemy territory where women and boys and girls and old men were being raped by soldiers

I made it back to my family home intact, only to find it under armed guard and my father under house arrest, protesting his innocence as a businessman who wasn't a politician

I remember they let us go and we fled to a neighbouring country as refugees, where we were harassed by the police, and my father lived in fear of losing his Alien Certificate which would mean his imprisonment until he could miraculously re-produce it

I remember returning to our homeland when we thought it

was safe, but my father's house and businesses and assets had been seized

I remember my father fighting for the return of his property and being threatened with prison or execution

I remember watching how my father's spirit was crushed and his heart, in the end, stopped – and could not be revived

I remember fleeing the city again after another military flare-up and driving into an ambush of armed soldiers with leaves sprouting from their uniforms who sprayed our car with bullets killing my younger sister and I remember feeling so angry I wanted to be a soldier, to take my revenge

I remember my grandparents sent me to England to claim asylum when I was seventeen, and how later they too were arrested and killed

I remember missing all the people I had lost, but not having time or a peaceful place to grieve

I remember I'd already learned to hold my composure as if nothing was a problem and in this way got past the officials at the airport when they questioned my surname on my passport

I remember I was put in a caged van and taken to a prison on arrival in England

I remember that 30 years ago I was eventually granted asylum and given five pounds and told to make my way on my own to an accommodation address in east London to start the process of proper resettlement

I remember I became a social worker specialising in young asylum seekers because I had been one myself – the eighteen-year-olds who are locked up in detention centres, the sixteens and younger who are placed in foster care

I know that the correct assessment of a young person's age can be key to their treatment, application and ultimately their survival

I know the Vietnamese and Afghans often look younger than their age, and the Eritreans older

I know that a child who has suffered terrible trauma can come across as an adult, as opposed to an adult who is pretending to be a child

I know that Egyptians pretending to be Syrians are usually caught out through language analysis

I know the Vietnamese young people who arrive here are quickly trafficked into cannabis factories, nail bars, or end up as sex slaves, so we urgently place them in foster care for their own protection

I know that adrenaline keeps my young people going on their journey, but once they reach their destination – are given food and shelter – then and only then does the magma rise through the cracks in their defences, and the lava overflows, which is a phenomenon to behold

I know a young person so wild and damaged that he attacked me, and others try to take their own lives because they cannot live with what they have been through, and some succeed

I know a young person sectioned because he was so violent he needed injections to stabilise him on a Treatment Order, yet still the government insisted he was pretending and used that against him to deny him asylum – which we got overturned on appeal, of which I am proud

I know that immigration law boils down to discretion and while the evidence might be bulletproof to everyone concerned, the judge might decide otherwise

I know that resources and local advocates in the community for citizen children in care are not so available when you have an asylum child, who is seen as an inconvenience

I know that the asylum interviews are intense and meticulous and the refugee applicant has to be mentally prepared to withstand the pressure

I know that as their social worker I can make all the difference to a young asylum seeker staying or being sent back

I know I have to help my young people tell their stories, so that they can state their case successfully when under interrogation

I worked with a young Muslim girl who would not even look at me, let alone talk to me, who would not see a therapist, who was definitely not going to get asylum, because her immigration statement was so sketchy it would be rejected outright

This young girl was so traumatised, her story could not even come out of her mouth, and I was her only hope so I had to get to know her slowly, to coax her, get her to trust me, and only then did she open up

This girl had to look after her sick mother instead of attending school and in Eritrea, most sixteen-year-olds are conscripted into the army for an indefinite period – five years, ten, twenty, but if you are younger and not in school, they will force you into the army earlier

So this one girl was fourteen years of age and her absence was reported to the authorities by the school administrators and she was rounded up and taken into the army where she had to sleep on the floor and was sent to do slave labour on a farm

This girl was advised by the older girls who had been there a long time to escape if you can, anything is better than this place where you have no future and no normal life and there are many more men than women and if they do not rape you straight away, they will soon drag you out at night and share you around

So this girl was strong in her mind and decided she had already lost her liberty so escaping was worth the risk, she plotted with another girl to run away when they collected firewood in the forest, a whole day's activity of chopping it down and loading it into trucks, at risk of being caught and killed, or caught and locked in a container in the blazing heat for days, or being caught and gang-raped by male soldiers, but this was going to happen anyway

This girl and the other one started running when the soldiers guarding them were sitting down having a midday nap, they'd been told that nobody could escape the camp because of the hostile landscape out there, but she didn't care and they ran and ran and ran and ran and when they could run no more they walked and walked and walked and walked into the depth of the night and into the next day, expecting the guards to come after them, but they did not

So these two girls walked and walked and walked some distance from the main road heading towards Ethiopia, relying on the good will of the local people, then she walked along the border with Ethiopia and got caught up in what she described as a wave of people doing the same thing, walking on into Sudan where she was told there was a high risk of being snatched by bandits as they crossed the desert squashed up in a truck and were stopped by police or soldiers, she wasn't sure which, who were paid a bribe and searched every part of the females including putting their hands inside them, inside her, defiling her

And once this girl reached Libya it was a point of no return, she said, you don't have a choice to go back as one smuggler hands you to the next and she was kept there in some kind of dungeon by men who were beasts, and if they had no use for you, no prospect of getting ransom money, they shoot you, if you are a woman with child, they leave you alone, the rest of the females were theirs for the taking and they forced her to pay for her passage across to Italy by forcing themselves on her many times with no protection and no hygiene, until she was not young anymore

This girl was there two months until they collected her in the middle of the night, she was not allowed to speak, they drove her to the sea, put her on a boat, she crossed into Italy and joined another wave of people on the move and made it to Calais where she waited three months before coming to England in the back of a lorry

I knew the challenge was how to make this girl a credible witness to her own persecution in front of asylum officials and interviewers determined to catch out this poorly educated fifteen-year-old village girl fresh from her troubles and nowhere near recovered

I knew the challenge was that the asylum caseworkers are overloaded and have to meet targets and have no time or patience for asylum seekers who are not able to express themselves well

I knew I had to support this girl's mental state to the point where she could have a thought process bearable enough for her to be able to recount her story to the solicitor I got for her, with me sitting there supporting her over a number of sessions, sometimes waiting or ending the session when she broke down into tears, knowing she was being forced to relive the horrors of her journey

I knew that if she could tell her story succinctly and fluently at the substantive interview without having a panic attack, where her body would go into uncontrollable spasms, or clamming up, she had a chance of getting through on the basis of her human rights claims

I am pleased to say that this girl is now eighteen and living in a supported family setting which might last until she is 25, it was a tough negotiation with management because it is very expensive, but I said to them, if you cast this girl out to live alone she will not survive, she has too much trauma, you might as well put her in a dingy in the middle of the Mediterranean and turn it upside down

I am pleased to say that this girl now understands that not every woman in the world has had FGM, something she thought was true when she told me the story of being held down by a group of women when she was six years old to have her private parts butchered

I am pleased to say that my job helping young people is the greatest reward, making sure their stories are told and meet human rights criteria when they do not even understand the meaning of it, but have lived through some of the world's worst atrocities

I have worked with boys of fourteen, fifteen, who are so worried they have AIDS and when you ask them why, having already noticed how sexualised and feminised they are, they cannot tell you

I see myself as someone who has known the terror of tyranny and the suffering of a deep loss, of losing my family, of losing my country, of starting over again in a place where I was a complete stranger with no one to guide me, no one to help me through a difficult system

I see myself as someone who goes to work every day knowing I am doing good in the world, and that I am working with the young people I can help the most, the young people who have the disadvantage, like me, of being born in the right country at the wrong time.

The Expectant Mother's Tale

as told to

Jonathan Skinner

THE TALE WAS TOLD, it was heard, and recorded, over the Internet. One did not see the teller but heard her tale. Two people, two migrants living on different parts of the island, from opposite ends of the world, brought together for the telling of this tale. One was hired, sponsored, screened, fingerprinted, photographed, admitted, employed, surcharged, renewed, paid monthly, counselled, processed, finally granted leave to remain. This one listened, transcribed, edited. One fled with the person she loved, who had to flee, was sent here, detained, fell pregnant, an expectant mother in prison, suffered for the child, for herself, was finally released, sent to her part of the island to wait, where she gave birth, not once but twice, but where she still waits. This is her tale.

My husband and I left our country some years ago. I did my Masters then worked for a multinational in my home country for three years, and then I got an opportunity to go abroad. I was interviewed for a manager's position in a government company specialised in making animal feed and consumer products. They wanted to employ somebody who could fill a recruitment position, so they hired me and I left my country for almost two years and it was difficult because my husband was back home and I was not happy away from home and family. I got married and decided to return home, and then I started working for another company, and my husband started having some problems at work and we had no options and we discussed it with our church, and it was getting very difficult for my husband to be there.

I didn't want to leave because I had a good job, we both had very good jobs, and we were doing very well, but because I had no option, I left with my husband, and we went to the low countries, that's where we did our asylum. But because my husband had connections with the government back home, and he had travelled many times to the UK, when we went to the low countries they interviewed him under the Dublin convention, and they said the UK was responsible for my asylum and not the country we had landed in, so we were there for four months. And then the Home Office accepted that the UK was responsible for me, to process my application here, and so they told us that we both had to go to the UK. We didn't even understand what they were talking about. They said we had to go, and they detained us in the low countries.

The authorities had discussed it with the UK authorities and finally they decided to send us here, but it wasn't that easy, just to send us here, because we did not want to come here, and we didn't know what would happen when we came here, probably they might just send us back home, while detaining us here, they could do that. We could understand that things might not be all right then. Even in the place we landed in the low countries, some of the officers who were very kind to us said: we don't know what they will do with you, but the chances are they will try to send you back to your country. And we can't go back, so they used force on my husband and brought him here and they still kept me there and then after some weeks they also got me here.

My husband was in detention, yes, and I had to follow, because that was how they broke us emotionally, they separated us. However, we came here, and when I came to the airport I just said that I want to be with my husband, and they said, all right, there was a good officer, and he said, I'll try to see what I can do for you and I will try to put you together, and I said you should set us free now, and he said, no, you will be detained, and I said why, and he said, ah, we have to detain you, and I said, but we haven't done anything wrong, the European authorities have sent us here and you should release us and they said, no, we will send you to detention too, and so they took me to a detention centre and we were there together. For six months, from the spring into the fall.

They had to bring us here on a flight, with the police, that was not a good experience, I've forgiven, but it wasn't a pleasant experience, to come with police and people staring at you. When they united us, they had this plan to send us back, so the Fast Track officers on our case refused us, and then kept giving us tickets on charter flights, and it was difficult, because we knew that we had a good case, but it seemed that things were not happening for us, and, well, they Fast Tracked our case, so they just did everything very quickly, and said that, obviously, it would take time to get travel documents. We didn't leave with documents, we left for life, you see, we had problems, we had to leave. Things were not happening for us and it seemed that they were just making it difficult for the two of us.

I fell pregnant, and then it became more difficult, it was my first pregnancy, I was very ill, and I had severe morning sickness and I couldn't be in detention, but they said, no, you will have to be in detention. From early spring into the fall we were in detention. And then we got hold of a good firm, a good solicitor, who said, why have you been here for that long, this is not *right*, your detention is unlawful, you shouldn't have been detained, and he took our case on.

Nothing helped, because they said being pregnant is not a sickness, you have to be here, and there were times I fainted while I was inside. They have a little canteen, a small shop where you could buy things, and I went there, and said, I'll just take some strawberries, and take some coconut water, and keep myself hydrated, but I did not like the food. And while I was in the queue, I said, I'm feeling very sick, and they said they thought I was acting up, they thought I was just being dramatic, and then, in fact, I fell, I collapsed, and I didn't know where I was, and at that point they rushed me to the health care centre, and said, well, why didn't you come to us. I said, I did come to you, earlier, saying that I am feeling awful, I am feeling sick. But you said there was nobody to look at me.

So things became very difficult from then, and the local visitor and befriending group helped me to get in touch with Medical Justice, and they said, you need medical help, you need proper care, because it's your first pregnancy, and so they made an arrangement to come and see me, with a midwife, and said, you need to go for a scan. There wasn't proper care, there is a health care department, but they really don't help you that much, they just tell you to take a Paracetamol if you don't feel that well, but they don't treat you, and to get appointments with the doctors there takes a while. Even with food, they had timings. I wouldn't want to have my breakfast at seven in the morning, but I had to force myself to wake up and go and have breakfast so that I felt better and felt well for the baby. Then there were timings for lunch, and on certain days I didn't want to have lunch at that time, but I had to force myself to go for lunch, to eat the same food every day. You had a menu, and you could decide what you wanted to eat, you had to decide for a week in advance, so it was just the same food. They would serve you chips and burgers and paninis. I am actually vegetarian, so they would serve me vegetable curry. I just didn't like it, and rice, boiled rice every day, not nice, and chicken, I would be sick with the smell of chicken, and fish. It was hard, but nevertheless, there were good officers who would try to help, saying, all right, we could give you a bottle of milk, you could have milk during the day so you feel better. Then every day eating the same food, just apples, pears and bananas, that was our life, just eating fruit.

I kind of hate fruits now. During Ramadan, they would serve watermelon, and that is something that I love eating, it's nice, it's one of the lovely fruits, and sometimes they would give us two pieces of watermelon, and one day I went with my husband, and I asked, could he have two pieces, and he would share it with me, because I would crave watermelon, and one of the officers said, no, I can't give you so much, no. He wasn't a good officer. There are good and bad people everywhere, as you know. So there would be good officers who would help and say, all right, you can have an extra yoghurt, whereas sometimes some officers would say, no, you can't even have one, saying there won't be enough for others, but they wouldn't understand what it is to be pregnant and need extra food, and I was so weak, I was already underweight, and these things were difficult but we moved on, and in the fall we were released.

The befrienders are people who help, who come and visit you, if you don't have anybody in the country, or if you don't have friends, and we don't have family here, we have nobody in this country, so they said we will arrange for somebody to come and visit you, and that's how we could have somebody to talk to, because detention is like a prison. So, it wasn't easy, and the Medical Justice people got in touch with me, and they came and visited me, and by that time, the solicitor that I just mentioned said we are going to have a bail hearing for you and try to get you out of detention, and so they had a bail hearing, and after nearly six months the judge called us, and the Home Office people were there and said, why have you been there for that long, and then my barrister argued that we were detained unlawfully, and finally the judge said, you need to release this couple, you kept them there for too long, for no reason, and they have a case pending now, and they should be released. And so we came out of detention then.

The day they said that you are released, they just told us, we were not even mentally prepared, that they would release us today, and they said, just quickly pack up, in an hour's time, pack up your stuff and come to the reception. However, we went there, and we had to call this friend of ours, the befriender, and she came to pick us up, took us to her place, we left all our stuff at her place, and just took one suitcase, and they gave us a train ticket to go to the city, and we got there at night, at around ten o'clock, there was no room for us, they said, there's no room here, and what do we do now, and they said, sit at the reception, we will send you to another bed and breakfast, so at around twelve, or one in the morning, we got sorted with a room.

Then for two weeks we were in accommodation in the city and then after that things really became more difficult, because we didn't have an address, and you know if you don't have an address here the GP won't see you, so I was due another scan then, and because I didn't have an address, a permanent address, I just had to go to walk-in clinics, and they said we can only have a look at you and that's it, but I still wasn't getting proper medical attention. And then I just got so frustrated with the system, the way things work in this country, but because I have a very strong belief in Jesus I kept that belief, and I kept that trust in him, and one day I just went for a very long walk and I said I'll put it in the Lord's hand and I will make a call to the Home Office today and tell them that I need a scan, I need a house where I can live till I hear on my case, and apparently I got in touch with a good officer and he said all right give me an hour's time and I'll try to sort things out for you, and he called back after an hour and said, I have an apartment for you, it's quite far away.

We were in the city at some accommodation, I don't even remember where it was, it's five years back, it was a bed and breakfast place, and people at that bed and breakfast already had letters from the Home Office saying that, you know, within two weeks' time, within a week's time, you will be moved to Birmingham, to Manchester, to other cities, and I said, I have nothing, I don't know what I'm going to do here, and then this officer called and said, all right, you be ready tomorrow morning, and somebody will come and take you, and I said, but I don't have any letter, I don't have any information, and he said, you just wait at the entrance with your husband, pack up your stuff and somebody will take you. And so we landed here.

And then we had proper healthcare, you know, treatment, had a GP, had hospital visits, and so we are still waiting to hear on our case, as I mentioned, we were put on Fast Track, if you know about Fast Track, there have been court hearings, and so, people who were on Fast Track, their cases are taking a bit of time, because all of those cases are in the Supreme Court right now, so we have to wait for a decision to come on that, whereas about my unlawful detention, my lawyers are working on it, and it seems that hopefully things will go in our favour, but it's just a matter of time, to wait and see what happens. It seems that hopefully, God willing, we will get sorted.

Being detained has had a very bad impact on my life, it's something I cannot forget, I haven't ever told this to my family. There were times when I was in detention, my family said, come online, and, you know, get on Skype, and my mom would say, I want to see you, and I would say, well, I'm busy, and, I don't have a phone here, and I would tell her, you can't come, and she would say, is everything all right, and I would say, yeah, everything is all right. And all those months I didn't even tell her where I was, so it has had an impact on my life, and it upsets me when I have to talk about it. My daughter is four now, and I don't think I plan to tell her.

I cannot express what it is to be there, it is hard to explain every situation, every moment, every minute, what you feel when you are there, for something that you have not done, it's like a spot on you that nobody can erase. Even if I get sorted it will still be there, you know, that experience, it's something that just keeps coming back. I don't plan to tell the story to my daughter, maybe when she's big enough and she can understand what a detention centre is, and when she's in school and understands these kind of things, maybe then, but for now I don't plan to tell her anything, but she's smart.

Last year my mom passed away and I emotionally broke down. I was planning, once I got sorted, to go and see my mom, and I wanted to see her, it had been such a long time, but that day didn't come, and she died last year. It was hard because I had not seen her for such a long time, and I was just waiting to hear some good news on my case, but didn't hear anything. So we had made a friend, a befriender, and that lady used to come every week to talk to us, and she came over on that day, it was a Friday morning when I got the news from back home, and she immediately said, I'm coming, I'll be there in three hours' time, and she came. She's in touch with me now too, and my daughter calls her grandma, she's actually her grandma, her UK grandma, she says I've adopted her as a grandma, you know, and she's kept in touch with us ever since we came out, ever since we were inside. And she said that my daughter is her first grandchild, and so, yes, she says that she's her special girl, my daughter is all for her. The befriender is a Christian, but she doesn't practice her faith, but I tell you, it's not necessary that you have to be religious to help people, what's the use of being religious when you don't have a heart to help. She, on the other hand, doesn't practice, but she is a good person and she helped us and said, you know, wherever you are, I'll keep visiting you once a month.

Because of the background that I have, I'm a very social person, so when I was in detention, I would make sure to help people, to read for them in English, or to help them if they needed help with forms, any way we could help. There was one officer, he said, one day you will be out of this place, because of your good behaviour, your good attitude. And I said, I don't think so, how is my good behaviour and attitude going to help me? The Home Office doesn't know what I am doing, how we are helping people to read documents who can't read a word of English. And he said, take my words, one day you will be released just because of your positive attitude and your helping attitude towards other detainees. And those words of that man came true, and we were released. If you are a Christian, then just remember us, and pray for us, so that one day I can call you and say, we are sorted, and we are free.

The Parent's Tale

as told by

J

Immigration! Immigration!! Immigration!!!

Sitting at the back of the van, the immigration van, it all seemed like I was daydreaming. Handcuffed, all alone, with an iron door and no window, I was speechless, in a state of shock. My heart was racing and I started having flashbacks.

My name is J and I am from West Africa. It's a privilege to be able to share my story and expose the hidden system of indefinite immigration detention in the UK. I had come to the UK in the year 1996 because I was being persecuted and tortured for my religious beliefs. I am from a Muslim background but converted to Christianity. As a result, I experienced persecution, false imprisonment and torture.

When I got to the UK I was very naïve, like any other immigrant with no previous exposure to the facts of living abroad. Those first few years were so tough, and I had to find a way to find a job and make money. In the process, I had my first encounter with the State and with Immigration (the UKBA) in 2004. I was put in a police cell for 24 hours. I attended a court hearing the next day, handcuffed, and thereafter put in a van and driven all the way to a detention centre, again in handcuffs. I felt so depressed and disorientated being locked in a box in a special van. The space was so tight you could barely stretch your legs. There was no window and no soundproofing. I was detained for just over two weeks and then released because of a medical condition. That experience has stayed with me to this day, like every other experience with the UKBA and Immigration over the years. In total, I have been detained five different times for a period of two years. I was treated just like a criminal for trying to obtain a job.

That was the beginning of my journey with the UKBA. After being released, I stayed with my uncle for a few years. Upon release, I was instructed to report to the immigration centre in Croydon. Despite having no form of income or support, I was still expected to turn up on a weekly basis. I struggled financially, and when, one time, I failed to report I became terrified that the next time I reported I would be re-detained. My first experience of detention had scared me so much I didn't dare report again. As a result I lost all contact with the UKBA for years until they encountered me a second time, in 2009. This time I was arrested and sentenced to eight months imprisonment for trying to obtain a job. It was one of my worst experiences. During my sentence, I was transferred all over the country from one prison to another. It was a real torture. I was completely numb. It felt like I was in a bad dream. I spent time in three different prisons. I was completely drained and very unstable mentally. In one prison, I shared a room with people who had committed very serious crimes. It was a whole new experience for me. I was at my wits' end. Throughout all this, my wife stood by me, travelling down to visit me even though she had no form of income herself, as her own application was pending with the Home Office.

In December 2010, I finished my sentence and was moved to the immigration removal centre at Dover. There, I was detained for six months. It was very regimented, similar to prison, with the officers treating detainees much like prisoners. Sometimes, if a detainee was given a removal direction, officers would try to block or frustrate their attempts to prepare the paperwork that might stop the order or the flight that followed. Some officers were not very professional and some stated personal motivations, saying, 'Britain is a small island and we don't need more people.'

I was released on bail in July 2010 and instructed to report three times a week at Croydon reporting centre, again with no form of support, work or income. While reporting in August 2010, I was detained. Myself and other immigrants were kept till evening at the reporting centre before being moved to a detention centre next door to an airport. We didn't get checked into the centre until about midnight. The process was always very tiring, even for the officers, not to mention the detainees. I thought, *here we go again*. Even though I complied with reporting I still got detained. It's almost like no matter what you do, you are likely to be detained in any case. This time I met a chap at the reporting centre who was arrested during his wedding ceremony with his wife, a British lady. It was surprising as their marriage was not an arranged one but Immigration said they suspected it was arranged. The chap was so heartbroken. He had to leave the UK but his British wife went to join him in Africa. The immigration system is so biased that they punish their own citizens as well as others to get immigration figures down at all cost.

I was in detention for a further nine months. It felt like forever. These kinds of experiences left many people mentally unwell and needing long-term medication. What the UKBA strategy does is break you. I witnessed many detainees losing their mind, but in most cases the officers at the centre think detainees are acting up. I have witnessed a blind person being detained and then, when he applied for bail, the judge determined he was going to abscond – the 'flight risk' argument being the most common weapon used by Immigration and UKBA. This is not to mention students being detained the moment they land at the airport, their studies abandoned, their student visas cancelled, even their hard-earned scholarships withheld by their universities, in the process. I saw all sorts and I began to understand how mental torture can be a very subtle thing; invisible but something you can carry like a scar for the rest of your life.

I have to say that those days were agonising, seeing families separated and lives destroyed. Once you are inside a detention centre you lose almost all your rights. Even writing about my experiences isn't easy for me. During my time in detention, I witnessed fellow detainees being woken in the middle of the night and moved to other detention centres, for no reason, and made to pack up all their belongings while still half-asleep. This can be very depressing, not knowing where you are being moved to, or why, and it being the middle of the night.

I tried to occupy my time and so, as well as going to the chaplain, I applied for work. It was too ironic. I was sentenced to prison and then detained for trying to obtain a low-paid job to sustain myself, but in detention I was offered a job with no National Insurance, at the rate of £1 per hour. I was finally granted bail in May 2011, after being represented by Bail for Immigration Detainees (BID). It was such a relief but stepping into the outside world now seemed strange to me. This whole experience also affected my wife, who was now on medication.

Some time after my release, my wife and I were blessed with a beautiful baby girl but during my wife's pregnancy, UKBA did everything possible to detain me. The way it seemed, this was because our case was getting stronger because of our family. Then in November 2013, I was arrested at home for failing to report on two occasions, despite having entirely justifiable reasons for missing these dates. The UKBA came to our address and arrested me in front of my wife and little girl, who was just one and a half years old. I was handcuffed and driven to detention again. My wife is still traumatised by this experience and over the following months our daughter became withdrawn and lost a lot of weight due to lack of appetite. She was especially close to me and now was so confused, not knowing where her daddy was. How could you explain that to her? My daughter was so close to me because I was primarily responsible for her care when she was born, as my wife had complications during and after her pregnancy.

These events really broke me from the inside. I felt so helpless, but God, my God, sent help: people like Don, who felt the immigration system and the hostile environment policy was inhumane, people like Sue and Christa. These people rose and fought with us without getting tired, and stood by us through the grace of God. I was detained for almost two months this time around. Removal directions were set and flights booked, but everything was reversed thanks to God, my wife and our helpers. Again, I was represented by BID and I was released. During my time in detention, my wife visited regularly with our daughter. After each visit, when I had to return to my cell, my daughter always wanted to come with me. That would break my heart. It was a detention centre and she was not allowed.

Getting bail from detention is always a big fight, especially if you have been criminalised. In all my experiences, I can say that I applied for bail up to seventeen times, but it was invariably rejected. This is because the Home Office will always paint you in such a bad light when it comes to your court hearing. Their first tactic is to say you will abscond; or they will book a removal direction for you the moment you apply for a court hearing, so that they can tell the judge that they have already arranged for your removal. There is so much I can say about the malpractices, treatment of immigrants and abuse of human rights in detention centres, but let me summarise it in one word: immigration detention is a *demonising* system.

After my release, I was signing on, or reporting, for a year when I was detained again while attending the reporting centre in Croydon. I had my daughter with me and my two sureties. We were supposed to be attending a bail renewal together with my wife. While in the centre, I was told that I needed to attend an interview, but right away I knew they wanted to detain me. I had been told the same thing a few years back while reporting, but on both occasions I was re-detained. This is one of their methods and I knew right away they were up to their usual game. My two sureties were shocked that the UKBA could be so deceptive, telling them it was a bail renewal. They couldn't believe what they saw at the reporting centre and the whole UKBA performance. To cut the story short, I was detained and as they handcuffed me my daughter was handed to my wife. This time I only spent two weeks in detention, before being released after being represented by BID. The flight was booked but cancelled by Judicial Review.

Finally, in 2016, a local charity referred my case, and my family's case, to a barristers chambers in London. Letters from friends, health professionals, and various organisations were presented along with our case, and finally my family and I were granted Leave to Remain in the UK. It has been a long journey, but thanks be to God who always gives us the victory. I use this opportunity to thank everyone who stood by us through this journey. God bless you all for your enduring support and care.

The Pruner's Tale

as told to

Lytton Smith

Come October, there will be apples piled in farmers' markets and kitchens across Western Upstate New York. There will be apple pies in ovens made with apples the Pruner has husbanded from sap to sprout to fruit. Pies from orchard apples, pies as American as, well, apple pie.

These past eighteen years, here in the US, more than half his life, the last eight at the orchard attached to the cider mill, the Pruner has learned the language of apples. Jonagold, Honeycrisp, Cameo. Thinning, spraying, suckers.

He's learned to cut back trees based on the varietal more than the season. He's learned chemicals that protect apples from fungi, learned how not to get sick from the chemicals. He's learned to tend to the sap when it's dormant, to cut back the tree at the right time for a kick of sweetness, a blush of colour. He's learned how a day like today, warm enough for short sleeves unless the breeze gets up, means it's too late to trim.

I love being outside, the Pruner says, being in touch with nature, contributing to putting fresh produce on other Americans' tables.

The thing to remember is, this might be the last season he does any of this.

He's expecting to be gone, come summer, though he won't say so in case saying makes it so. He's expecting to be gone, come summer, back to the Mexico he travelled from, back to the Mexico he's not seen since puberty, since fourteen. Back where his father was shot seven times with a 9mm. And survived. Survived three more years, survived in pain long enough to need a wheelchair, and medicine, and care.

And what does a family of twelve children, and a mother without a job, do with that? What can they do in a village that's not even really a village, more some houses near a mountain in Mexico's south-west?

★

The Pruner's house is out past steely solar farms, near the one-room white wooden church, opposite one field of the apple orchard. His nearest neighbours are a hefty baseball throw away.

The bonnet of an SUV hides him from view, at first. He pulls off medical-blue rubber gloves to talk. Fetches a bottle of Windex to clean a bug-spattered glass table two feet in diameter. He asks his daughter to fetch two chairs, which sink into a soil soft with the promise of spring. The soil, the Pruner will say, is why immigrants come here: it's rich, the area's rich in agriculture.

The thing to remember is, this might be the last season he does this. Outside with his children as winter yields to spring. Setting out the table: spray, wipe, spray, wipe. A smile – he smiles easily – and a hand, open in invitation.

He's been working at fixing the timing belts on the family car. It's a job that might take a day or so but it's been two weeks already. Yesterday, he was working from seven to seven, trying to get winter pruning done before the warmth; other days, it's seven to five. He has to set down his tools to remember the journey that brought him here. By the time he's finished talking, it's still light, the moon visible in the April sky adding to the evening's surprising brightness.

He'll have to go inside for dinner, for his kids' bedtimes.

The timing belts won't get fixed, not tonight. The car's going nowhere. With his car out of action, the Pruner has to hope he's assigned to work in a field to which he can walk. Sometimes, he's assigned to a site five miles away, ten miles away. He pays someone $20 a day to drive him; he works six days a week, and soon that's $120.

Before he was pulled over by the police, before the nights in the Buffalo Federal Detention Facility – which isn't in the city of Buffalo but a small rural town, Batavia, one more veil that makes it harder to find the detained – before the deportation hearing that was postponed because of the shutdown over whether the President could build the wall to keep out those 'bad hombres' from Mexico, before all this, there was a time he didn't drive anywhere.

You have to stay hidden, he explains, the underside of his voice furred with an anger as fine as the hairs on an apple leaf. There are eyes on you, if you're Mexican. Law enforcement. ICE – Immigrations and Customs Enforcement – racists. People who don't like you. He repeats that word often, *hidden*. That is what it means to be undocumented, the Pruner says. You have to keep moving house, he says; if you don't, they might find you. Border patrol. ICE. One year, move on.

But you start raising a family, start having children. You find yourself in need, he says, of operating a vehicle. It matters that he says it that way: you find yourself in need. Of going to the doctor. Of taking your babies to daycare. Your child is sick, how are you going to collect them from daycare? 'Papa,' your eldest says, 'I want to join the soccer team. Papa, why don't you take us camping, why don't you take us to a State park?'

The Pruner was headed to the pharmacy when the officer pulled him over. He didn't have a licence to hand over, because that's what being undocumented means. No licence, no way to get a licence. Stay hidden. The Pruner hands over a Mexican identification card, as if it's better to prove he's documented somewhere, even if that somewhere is a past that once left him so famished he'd felt his spine through his stomach.

We're going to see some friends, is how the officer puts it. The Pruner's up against his own car, hands cuffed behind his back. He knows friends means ICE, ICE means detainment, detainment might mean deportation. The moment the officer pulls him over, the Pruner becomes *removable*. Undocumented, so removable. The medicine, for his child's bronchitis, lost to the day.

In detention, he's given three minutes' worth of credit. Three minutes to call his wife and hope she, not his children, answer. Three minutes to tell her he's in detention, she must find someone who can pay the thousands of dollars his bond will be so he can get bail, so he can go back to pruning the orchard, back to the apples needed for the pies and sauce and cider and juice and lunchboxes of Western Upstate New York. Back to waiting for deportation.

What the three minutes – they're almost up – won't allow is for him to tell anyone what brought him here aged fourteen. Here, at first, was Arizona, maybe New Mexico, somewhere he wasn't long enough to really recall – somewhere he stumbled to, across the Sonoran desert, having paid a man to get him to the desert, indenturing himself. Somewhere he was taken from instantly for Florida, for strawberries. 'So you guys can pay, the man said, 'pay us by working strawberry fields.' New Year's Eve, 2000, the Pruner was in Mexico; New Year's Day, 2001, in the United States. 'I had to lie, of course, so they'd give me a job, say I was eighteen.'

Three minutes are up, but there's more to tell. He left school at twelve, or was it ten, sixth grade, left his friends playing soccer so he could work full-time at a construction site where he dislocated his back lugging 50 kilos of cement. Where he watched his old friends from the site and first felt the loneliness that wouldn't leave him anywhere in Mexico.

Perhaps his journey didn't begin with the crossing of the border, or his father being shot, or his leaving school; perhaps it began with the loneliness.

Or perhaps his journey began with need, with hunger.

One night, the Pruner remembers, not wanting to remember, his mother didn't have corn to cook overnight so she'd be able to make tortillas in the morning. There wasn't ever anything much to go with the tortillas, supposing there were tortillas: beans, if they were lucky; tomato, maybe; more likely, salt. But they weren't lucky: tonight, there wasn't corn to make tortillas, and there were seven of them, mother and six children. The other siblings had left. Leaving meant not being a mouth to feed with the tortillas there weren't any of.

The Pruner can't say how his mother slept that night, without food for her children. She set off first thing in the morning to ask the neighbours for food she'd repay down the line. No one had any, until she came to the neighbours who'd just finished their fill of a dozen or so, piping hot. Her timing all wrong.

We have, they told her, sorry to offer, the tortillas for the pig. You can have those.

The tortillas for the pig: the extra tortillas, the uneaten surplus. Tortillas from a week back, a month, maybe more. His mother accepts them, a bag of twenty or so. She brings them home. Her children are hungry and wondering and they watch her wash tortillas with her rag, wash mould off tortillas fit for a pig. Wash, and scrape, and scrape, and wash.

She gets the fire going, and when the tortillas are as scrubbed as they'll get, she cooks them crunchy, hot enough to singe but not burn. We have a meal, the Pruner says, tortillas with salt.

The Pruner, the boy who'll become the Pruner, knows if he can't make enough to feed himself and the rest, he needs to get going. He tries heading up to the mountain, where the town will let him have a plot of land to grow what corn and beans he can. For months, he'll head there with his donkey and the dog he raised – the dog he found at three weeks old, the only dog that survived of the litter, the dog he nursed to life with masa and water, the dog he gives half his own food. He'll tend the land until two in the afternoon. From two to four, he'll gather firewood. At four, he'll head back down the mountain, so thin and so hungry he feels his stomach against his spine.

Three minutes passed a long time back. There's so much more to the Pruner's tale. Given another three minutes, he'd tell of the orange his aunt offered his mother, how his mother accepted it but didn't eat it, how she brought it home to her children. How they came around her like chicks around a hen, and she started peeling this orange. When she finished, her children sitting around her, she shared it out. One piece for you. One for you. A piece for you. One piece for you. A piece for you. And here, in Western Upstate New York, the Pruner rubs his hands together like a mother all out of orange pieces, like a mother whose hands are sticky with juice.

Maybe, who knows, that's where the Pruner's journey began. A through-line from a shared orange to a southwestern desert to a strawberry field to a decade of tended and gathered and picked apples. To a home 28 miles from the Canadian border. To a detention cell in a facility whose name locates it somewhere it is not. To deportation.

He's happy, he says, he helped put his siblings through school, working here so they didn't have to do what he'd done there. The construction site, the mountain farm, any more meals of spoiled tortillas.

The thing to remember is, this might be the last season he does any of this, the last season in this place he's made his home with his hands, grown his family.

The thing to remember is, for the three days and nights the Pruner was in Buffalo Federal Detention Facility, his wife didn't eat, didn't sleep. Didn't tell him, the times he borrowed other inmates' credit to call her, how she spent her time crying. He only finds out after, when he's back, when his daughter tells him.

★

This tale could – should – have been another tale. The Astronaut's Tale. That's what he wished to be, as a boy, before his father got shot and there were mouths to feed and he left school. The Biologist's Tale. The Chemist's Tale.

'I was so, so interested in elements, gravity, in life – studying molecules and cells, all the living creatures…I have that *in* me,' he says, earnest in the way no twelve-year-old boy is allowed to be earnest, not here, not in rural Mexico, not wherever this tale is being heard. He's leaning forward, the most animated he's been: 'I had a big, big wish to learn, to continue in school.'

This should have been the Wisher's Tale, for the Pruner never stops wishing. The thing to remember is this might be his last season, but he knows what he'd contribute if he could only stay. In his eyes as he looks out on to the orchard across the road, there's a repair shop. There's a restaurant, he says, serving authentic food from the region where he grew up, and his daughter will run it. A farm, too, he'd like that. He'd like to keep on growing. The soil is rich.

He doesn't want to go back, back to awkward adolescence, back to his father's death; there's nothing there for him, nothing to contribute. His oldest has reached seventh grade, one grade past when he left school to work construction to feed his siblings. There's nothing more he can teach her, he says, with that easy smile. She's in junior honours society and she just got an award for leadership. He's made sure she knows all the math he knows, long division, all that, what he can teach her about writing and reading. She's on her own now, he's told her, and he's wishing he'll get to be right there beside her.

He wishes, too, his mother could come meet his children. His mother hasn't met them, not any of them. She didn't, he says, hold his oldest in her arms as a baby, and now that child, she's almost a woman, almost grown up. He wishes there was a way his mother could be here.

Being undocumented, being removable: it means not being able to take journeys, it means this might be the last season he gets to do any of this, the schoolwork, the pruning.

Despite it all, he loves it here, here in Western Upstate New York, here where there's a town called Sweden and one called Somerset and another Bergen and one called Greece, and the wines tastes like German wines and have German names, and where the winds blow in across the border of the Great Lakes a Canadian cold, northern snow.

'Maybe my wife will tell my bosses one day,' he says, 'He's not here, he's been sent back to Mexico'. The Pruner pauses long enough for it to feel like the tale's told out. 'I love the United States. I got here when I was a child. I know I'm Mexican because I was born in Mexico. But I feel the United States is my home. Western New York has become my home. I'm feeling myself as Western New York. I'm feeling myself as United States.'

What are the words for when someone loves a place, and tends its crops, and raises a family, and finds a church, and prays, and prunes, and is told he's removable, that this land whose soil he's come to know can't be his soil?

★

Instead of the land giving rise to a language, instead of a vocabulary of apples, and pruning, and husbandry, human journeys get told and concealed in administrative terms. In words that have the force of speech acts, making things happen whether we want them or not. Leave to remain. Removable. Inadmissible.

There was a time, not long ago, the Pruner remembers, when he was highly valuable. A lawyer for the government said so. It was after he was pulled over, and before the election, and at his deportation hearing a lawyer who likely knew little of dormant sap and winter pruning made the case that the Pruner was providing labour that mattered to Western Upstate New York, mattered to the United States, that this type of person was worth having here. His deportation was administratively closed: neither endorsed nor refuted. Having detained him, the government was allowing him to return to a life of staying hidden.

What changed was the will of the people, the President's mandate. Under the new administration, the Pruner was once again removable. That is how language, which is to say bureaucracy, speaks people, and not the other way around.

'You are not free, here,' says the Pruner, 'if you are undocumented. We have a saying in Mexico, how the bird in a cage, even one made of gold, cannot fly and so is not free. You have to be able to move,' he says. 'You have to be free.'

★

Come fall, there'll be apples on tables, and the Pruner will have been part of that journey, but he might well no longer be here. He's removable, the administration says. He's undocumented, which means you stay hidden until you can't stay hidden. When you can't stay hidden you get deported, and who knows what happens to your family, your car with its broken timing belts, the orchard you've pruned the best part of a decade, the apples you'd planned you'd be picking.

The thing to remember is, this might be the last season he gets to do any of this, but he still loves it here. 'It's still been worth it,' he says. He keeps saying it. 'I have a family,' he says. 'I have stories, too many stories.' And he laughs. Is there such a thing, a job, like a storyteller?

Afterword

The Walk

Refugee Tales, as the subtitle has it, and as the project reiterates everywhere it goes, is 'A Walk in Solidarity with Refugees, Asylum Seekers and Detainees'. The purpose of the project is to call attention to the fact, to call out the fact, that the UK is the only country in Europe that detains people indefinitely under immigration rules, and in the process, as it walks, to call for that practice to end. The way the project makes that call is by sharing the stories of people who have experienced detention. The stories are told and heard in the context of the community that forms through walking. When Refugee Tales walks again, in July 2019, it will be for the fifth time.

The fact that this year the project will have walked for five years was not part of the original plan. That plan was formed by members of the Gatwick Detainees Welfare Group out of the shared frustration that, while for twenty years the Group's volunteers had visited people held in indefinite detention, the general public was barely aware that such a practice was being conducted in their name. Not only were the stories of those detained rarely, if ever, reported, but the fact that the UK practiced such detention was hardly known. Almost everything about detention and its consequences was rendered invisible. The practice could not be allowed to continue. Something had to change.

The plan, then, was to share the stories of people who had been held in detention, and to do so as part of an extended public walk. The idea was shared with groups working with people detained at the Dover Immigration Removal Centre – Kent Refugee Help and Samphire – and a route was developed that went from Dover to Crawley (the nearest town to the detention centres at Gatwick Airport) along the North Downs Way. That first walk lasted nine days, the aim being to create, in that act, a kind of spectacle of welcome and in so doing to help trigger the desire for change. Except that as people walked that first year it became clear that the project had no choice but to continue, that for at least two compelling reasons it couldn't stop.

The first reason was political. If the project was serious in its call for an end to indefinite detention, then it was clear that call would have to be made louder and for longer if it was to be widely heard. Refugee Tales was adding its voices to those of the many organisations and individuals who had been fighting for an end to indefinite detention for many years, and though the calls were intensifying inside and outside parliament it was apparent to everyone involved that more work had to be done. What was also clear, however, was that as people who had experienced detention walked with people who hadn't, so in that process a community formed. For everybody involved, albeit for different reasons and from different viewpoints, the walk constituted a space outside the hostile environment that, as Home Secretary, Theresa May had first set out to inflict on the UK in 2012.

For each of the following three years the project walked to Westminster: from Canterbury in 2016, from Runnymede in 2017, and from St. Albans via the East End of London in 2018. Everywhere it stopped it shared stories of people who had experienced detention with the general public, the venue frequently doubling as the space in which the project would collectively spend the night. At each evening event, the facts of detention would be reiterated and the audience would be called on to help communicate the urgency of the need for change, in particular to build pressure on a government in blatant breach of human rights. Then, during the walking day, with the stories from the night before giving rise to further stories, the project listened to talks outlining the need for and possibility of change. In 2017, for instance, the walk having started at the site of the signing of Magna Carta, a series of speakers considered the question of 'due process'. In 2018, to mark the document's 70th anniversary, talks took their lead from the Universal Declaration of Human Rights. Article 9 of the Declaration could not be clearer, 'Nobody shall be subjected to arbitrary arrest, detention, or exile', a basic provision of human protection with which the UK government is in conflict.

This year the Refugee Tales route runs from Brighton to Hastings, which means that as it makes its way the project will walk the border. Talks will consider what we need to do, in this moment of intensifying nationalism, to construct a politics capable of thinking beyond borders. Stories will convey the terrible damage done to individual lives by a border policy with indefinite detention at its heart. At the same time, however, as the project walks for a fifth year, so inevitably it will find itself contemplating how things have changed. And crucially, how they haven't; how the hostility continues, how the limbo in which politically vulnerable people find themselves goes on and on. There are people who first walked with Refugee Tales in 2015 whose situation hasn't altered: who still can't work, who are still forced to exist outside the cash economy, who still, at any moment, could find themselves re-detained. In 'The Voluntary Returner's Tale', told in 2016, Caroline Bergvall detailed the effect of slow violence. It is a form of violence the hostile environment was constructed to perfect.

The Hostile Environment

When Refugee Tales first walked in June 2015 the hostile environment was not widely discussed. In an interview with *The Daily Telegraph* three years earlier, Theresa May had announced the intention to use the Immigration Act of 2014 to create a 'really hostile environment for illegal migration'. The 2016 Immigration Act further intensified that hostility, with its root and branch foreclosure on anything like a livable life. At the same time, however, as official hostility to those seeking asylum has intensified, so also the Home Office's practices have become much more widely known and discussed, due not least to *The Guardian*'s reporting on the treatment of the Windrush generation. On a weekly basis news outlets now report new examples of official brutality against the politically vulnerable, of destitution, of detention, of deportation. The fact, however, that its policies are now relentlessly exposed can hardly yet be said to have altered Home Office behaviour. And seven years on from Theresa May's announcement of the government's intention we are still coming to terms with what the hostile environment has brought into effect.

The hostile environment, as the 2016 Immigration Act confirmed, is a sustained, systematic and brutal assault on every aspect of the life of the geo-politically vulnerable person. Denied the right to work for as long as their case is unresolved, which will frequently be for years and can easily be for well over a decade, a person seeking asylum finds their every movement compromised and controlled. As has been observed by Refugee Tales before, but which needs constant reiteration, such support as is afforded a person in that circumstance (at the subsistence level of £5 per day) is paid not in cash nor into a bank account (which since the 2016 Immigration Act it has been illegal for a person seeking asylum to hold), but as a voucher in the form of a top-up card that can only be spent on designated products at designated shops. This renders even the act of securing basic provisions a hostile process since the voucher – like a badge – has to be displayed at the point of transaction. It also subjects human movement itself to the process of hostility, since, as 'The Stateless Person's Tale' reiterates, public transport is not listed as an item on which the voucher might be spent.

One effect of this is that a person will spend endless hours walking, either to secure basic provisions, or to sign at a Home Office Reporting Centre, or because in the absence of work there is precious little else to do. And so the fact of moving, like the act of securing provisions, comes to carry the effect of the environment's hostility; an hostility intensified by the fact that at any moment the individual might (if they are in the unusually fortunate position of occupying Home Office accommodation) be relocated to another part of the country. The government's word for this is 'dispersal'. People frequently find themselves 'dispersed' – a process which has the consequence of breaking up such communities as they might manage to form. 'The Volunteer's Tale', published here, documents a series of officially sanctioned removals, removals that in his case, as in so many cases, follow a tragic history of exile and expulsion.

The hostility is intensified also, one should surely say fundamentally, by the fact that at any given moment (since the process is arbitrary) a person can be detained or re-detained. It is in this sense that the hostile environment has to be understood. Not simply (though this would be bad enough) as a set of bureaucratic procedures in which by accident or design an individual's future can get lost. But as a total space of existence in which the individual's personhood is shaped by hostility, as a condition in which personhood itself is systematically attacked.

As much, then, as the policies that constitute this assault on the politically vulnerable person are now known, still we are in the process of understanding their implications and political reach. Like any newly emerging normal, it takes time to realise what is at stake and it is perhaps helpful, as we continue to work out where we are headed, to offer three kinds of contextualising frame.

The first frame is historical and connects to the rise of the far right. One commentator people have consistently drawn on in trying to understand this connection is the German-

Jewish historian and philosopher Hannah Arendt. The importance of Arendt (who fled Germany in 1933, and German occupied-France for the USA in 1941) is that more clearly than any writer since the Second World War, she documented how the person who seeks asylum can find themselves abandoned between nation states. Thus her discussion of statelessness and rights in *Origins of Totalitarianism* (1950) remains unerringly accurate in its description of the vulnerability into which a stateless person can slip.

What has become apparent, however, in the past five years, as right-wing narratives of nation have gained sway in parts of Europe and America, is that we have to heed Arendt's warnings more closely and more urgently than we would have wanted to think. Thus, one thing Arendt was very careful to observe was the way administrative hostility could give way to, or could prepare the ground for, further large-scale assaults on personhood. As she put it, 'the methods by which individuals are adapted to these conditions, are transparent and logical.' Thus the insanity of the historical developments she was seeking to understand in *Origins of Totalitarianism* had its root, as she understood it, in administrative hostility, in the 'historically and politically intelligible preparation of living corpses.'

Arendt's history of totalitarianism was written in the form of a warning. Her aim was not to argue that one historical development follows straightforwardly or in any simple fashion from another, but that there are tendencies in politics by which we have to be alarmed. Thus when recently, under the Salvini Edict, the Italian government bulldozed the longstanding Castelnuovo di Porto refugee reception centre just outside Rome, evicting hundreds of refugees, the authorities were acting on grounds Hannah Arendt would recognise. The people concerned had been rendered so politically vulnerable as to make them subject, eventually, to state orchestrated violence. Understood historically, it is just such ground that UK policy makers began to prepare when they instigated the hostile environment. The intention was to produce an environment in which personhood itself could barely be sustained. The longer that environment exists, the more we understand its implications.

A second contextualising frame is indefinite detention itself. The fact that a person can be detained indefinitely is fundamental to the operation of the hostile environment as a whole. In part this is due to the permission the State grants itself once it allows itself to detain indefinitely. To detain a person in that way is to so fundamentally breach their human rights as to render them outside the provision of any such ethical framework. In order to detain indefinitely, in other words, the State must already have taken the decision that this is a person to whom rights don't apply. From which it follows that their personhood does not require respect. From which it follows that one can develop a comprehensively hostile space.

But it is not only a question of political permission. Indefinite detention underpins the hostile environment because it is the prospect of such arbitrary detention that instills the fear that shapes a person's relation to their everyday life. The number of people actually detained has remained stubbornly high through the past five years. The Home Office points to incremental reductions as a sign of improvement, but in the year ending December 2018, 24,748 people were detained indefinitely in the UK. Among the constants, in fact, of the past five years are the statistics around detention. Thus, of all those detained in that time, somewhere between 50 and 55% were released back 'into the community'. What 'community' means, in this context, is the situation described above, without work and where every movement is negatively managed. Still, though, since the Home Office's justification for indefinite detention is that it is preparatory to removal, then the fact that in the year ending December 2018, 55% of those detained were returned to the community shows that either detention is ineffective even in its own terms, or, alternatively, that its function is brutally symbolic.

Periods of detention continue to vary. Sometimes it will be for days, sometimes weeks, but still it can be for months and years. The longest Refugee Tales has known of a person to be detained indefinitely in the UK is nine years. At last count, and counting, the longest current period of detention was 744 days. In the year ending June 2018, ten people died while in detention and 159 people attempted suicide. To end indefinite detention would not be to end the hostile environment. It would, however, be to dismantle a fundamental aspect of its architecture.

A final contextualising frame is, as it were, geo-political. During the period that Refugee Tales has walked to call for an end to indefinite detention in the UK, the international use of detention as a political weapon has become increasingly widespread. The examples are numerous, from the Trump regime's separating of children and families in detention centres at the US–Mexican border, to the continued offshoring of detention by the Australian government, to the routine detention of political dissidents in Turkey. One could easily proliferate examples, and in doing so one could dwell on differences between political regimes. What needs to be understood, however, is that for all kinds of regime detention is an increasingly common default, and that therefore it has become one of the defining issues of our time. This makes it all the more crucial that detention is challenged locally wherever that challenge is necessary. What is required also, as Refugee Tales has increasingly argued, is an internationalised understanding of the detention regime. To contribute to that developing understanding, this volume includes an account of detention in the US context, with 'The Pruner's Tale' (as told to Lytton Smith), reporting on incarceration at the US–Canadian border. Detention is a global practice that increasingly defines geo-political space. It has to be confronted wherever it is practiced in the national context but also by networks working internationally.

Stories

One direct focus for the hostility of the hostile environment is the story of the person who seeks asylum. There are many ways this is the case. It remains a shocking fact that, as various organisations including Refugee Tales have reported, the bail hearing where an individual might be released from detention is not a court of record. This is true, also, of the deportation appeal hearing, on which occasion the individual's future security is at stake. While the judge will issue a determination, in which some account of the proceedings is given, there is no full transcript and therefore the words of the appellant are not on record. Consider also the fact that, in so far as the individual does present their story, that story is administratively weaponised against them. If, for instance, having first given an account of their experience in, say, 2003, and then, when called on twelve years later to account for the same experience at a different moment in the process, the person seeking asylum departs from their original telling in any way, then that divergence will be used to discredit the whole case. Or consider the fact, as R reports here, that one form of the asylum interview consists of an official asking approximately a hundred questions, and then, when they have finished, immediately asking the same hundred questions again. These processes do not simply silence, they turn the story against itself, weaponising the process of the narration such that the language itself is hostile.

That the asylum process demonstrates such hostility to a person's story, that it expends such energy discrediting and turning the story against itself, teaches us two things. In the first place what it surely shows is that the story itself is powerful, that where it is told and heard in its entirety it will have an altering effect. To tell and to hear a story, in other words, is to establish an intimate connection, a connection the hostile environment sets out explicitly to break. What that hostility to story also teaches, however, is that for the person whose status is not regularised and who is therefore variously vulnerable – to removal to the circumstance from which they fled, to detention or re-detention, to a process in which any variation between tellings might constitute a capital mistake – the sharing of the story is a potentially dangerous act.

It is for these reasons that the Refugee Tales project arrived at a collaborative model of storytelling, as a way of sharing the stories of people who had experienced indefinite detention which did not render individuals unsafe. At the same time, however, as the project has grown and developed, all manner of other modes of storytelling have emerged. The walk itself is one long, multiply-evolving set of stories, a mobile setting in which stories start up and intersect. It is a process that has gradually spilled out, so that as others have become interested in what Refugee Tales does, people who walk who have experienced detention have spoken in Parliament, to the BBC and to other broadcasters, and at festivals and events across the country. Increasingly also, as the space has come to seem secure, individuals have told their own stories to the audiences that gather at the walk's evening events, in particular when, after years of waiting, their status has finally been regularised. The first-person accounts of those people who wanted to have them published are presented here. Refugee Tales is profoundly grateful to everybody who has shared their story with the project, and to all those who have collaborated in the act of sharing.

Among the most brutal effects of the hostile environment, however, is precisely how, in so many cases, it does not allow a person's story to change. Simply put, in the five years that the Refugee Tales project has been in existence, the majority of those in the project who have experienced detention have seen no change in their post-detention life. Still they can't work. Still they are compelled to live outside a cash economy. Still each time they report their presence to the Home Office they face the prospect that they might be re-detained. 'The Stateless Person's Tale', as told to Abdulrazak Gurnah, reflects this ongoing situation, re-continuing, as it does, a collaboration that started in the first volume of *Refugee Tales*, and therefore documenting the human cost of the State's protracted violence. As urgently as indefinite detention has to be ended, so equally urgently people seeking asylum in the UK must be granted the right to work.

Political Change

Fundamental to the hostility of the hostile environment is the construction of a series of contexts in which those in authority feel no obligation to listen. 'The Volunteer's Tale' (as told by R), like all the tales collected here, documents the inhumanity of that reality. So concerned were the authorities to establish whether or not he had been fingerprinted in Italy, that they did not register the fact that he had been tortured in Libya and Sudan. It was only, as he says, when he was visited by a representative of the organisation Medical Justice that somebody actually stopped to listen.

Many organisations and many individuals over many years have sought to counter the official hostility of non-listening, as *Refugee Tales* has done through the medium of the public walk. What everybody involved has understood, however, is that the hostile environment itself has to change, that the practices by which it is sustained have to be ended. On the particular question of indefinite detention there is no doubt that political progress has been made. In 2015, the All Party Parliamentary Groups on Refugees and Migration reported on the 'Use of Immigration Detention in the United Kingdom' and concluded that, 'There should be a time limit of 28 days on the length of time anyone can be held in immigration detention.' In 2017 the British Medical Association and the Bar Council, reporting independently from their separate professional viewpoints, echoed the urgent need for such a limit. In 2018, making that need graphic, *Panorama* documented the shocking treatment of people detained at the Brook House Immigration Removal Centre. In March of this year, the Home Affairs Committee report on immigration detention found that 'Home Office policies... are regularly applied in such a way that the most vulnerable detainees, including victims of torture, are not being afforded the necessary protection' and echoed previous reports in calling directly for indefinite detention to end. All opposition parties committed to ending indefinite detention in their 2017 manifestos, while public support for legislative change has recently been communicated by various government MPs. The political argument, in other words, for an end to indefinite detention has unquestionably been won. The task now is to effect the change of law that reflects this new political reality.

Five years after the project began planning its first public walk, Refugee Tales continues to call out the fact that the UK is still, at the time of writing, the only country in Europe that detains people indefinitely under immigration rules. With each year that the project has walked, the more it has become clear just how systematic are the processes of the hostile environment, just how brutal is that environment's assault on the fundamentally vulnerable person. It is the power to detain indefinitely that underwrites the totality of that assault. Refugee Tales walks in solidarity with all those who call for that brutal practice to end.

David Herd
June 2019

About the Contributors

A currently resides in London. He is set to be a social work graduate and hopes to work as a social worker. He is also a writer of spoken word poetry. This is his first published story.

Monica Ali is the daughter of English and Bangladeshi parents. She came to England aged three, her first home being Bolton in Greater Manchester, and later studied at Oxford University. Her first novel, *Brick Lane* (2003), is an epic saga about a Bangladeshi family living in the UK, and explores the British immigrant experience. It was shortlisted for the 2003 Man Booker Prize for Fiction, and made into a film, released in 2007. Her second novel, *Alentejo Blue*, set in Portugal, was published in 2006, and her third, *In the Kitchen*, in 2009. Monica Ali lives in London and was named in 2003 by Granta magazine as one of 20 'Best of Young British Novelists'. Her latest novel is *Untold Story* (2011).

Lisa Appignanesi is a prize-winning author of fiction and non-fiction. She was President of English PEN and is currently Chair of the Royal Society of Literature. Her most recent book is *Everyday Madness: On Grief, Anger, Loss and Love*. Her many other works include *Trials of Passion: Crimes in the Name of Love and Madness*, *All About Love: Anatomy of an Unruly Emotion*, *Mad, Bad and Sad: A History of Women and the Mind Doctors*, and with John

Forrester, *Freud's Women*. She has written an acclaimed family memoir, *Losing the Dead*. Her novels include *The Memory Man* and the psychological thrillers *Paris Requiem* and *The Dead of Winter*. She writes for a variety of papers, including *The New York Review of Books* and broadcasts regularly on cultural themes. *Everyday Madness* was published in 2018.

B was granted definite leave to remain in the UK over twelve years after he first sought asylum. He graduated with a degree from a university in London and now works as a care worker in the West of England.

David Constantine was for 30 years a university teacher of German language and literature. He has published a dozen volumes of poetry, two novels and five collections of short stories. He is an editor and translator of Hölderlin, Goethe, Kleist and Brecht. With Helen Constantine he edited *Modern Poetry in Translation*, 2003-12. In 2018 Bloodaxe published his new and greatly enlarged *Selected Poetry of Hölderlin,* and Norton a *Collected Poems of Bertolt Brecht* translated by Tom Kuhn and him. He is a volunteer mentor with Refugee Resource.

Bernardine Evaristo MBE is the award-winning author of nine books of fiction and verse fiction including *Girl, Woman, Other* (Penguin 2019), *Mr Loverman* (Penguin, 2013), *Lara* (Bloodaxe, 2009), *Blonde Roots* (Penguin, 2008) and *The Emperor's Babe* (Penguin 2001). Her work includes drama and other writing for BBC Radio 3 & 4, as well as fiction, poetry, memoir, theatre drama and essays. She has judged and chaired many literary prizes and founded The Complete Works poetry development scheme for poets of colour in 2007, and the Brunel International African Poetry Prize in 2011. In 2004 she was elected a Fellow of the Royal Society of Literature; in 2006 she was appointed a Fellow of the Royal Society of Arts; and in 2017 she was elected a Fellow of the English Association. She is Professor of Creative Writing at Brunel University London.

F was granted leave to remain after nine and a half years seeking asylum, during most of which she lived in NASS accommodation. She has just finished the second year of her degree at a university in the south of England and is waiting to hear from the Home Office about the extension of her leave.

Patrick Gale is the author of the Emmy award-winning *Man in an Orange Shirt* and of many novels, including *The Whole Day Through, Notes from an Exhibition, A Perfectly Good Man,* the Costa-nominated *A Place Called Winter* and his latest *Take Nothing With You.* He was born on the Isle of Wight, where his father was prison governor at Camp Hill. His first two novels, *The Aerodynamics of Pork* and *Ease* were published by Abacus on the same day in June 1986. The following year he moved to Camelford near the north coast of Cornwall and began a love affair with the county that has fed his work ever since. He chairs the North Cornwall Book Festival, is patron of Penzance LitFest and a director of both Endelienta and the Charles Causley Trust.

Abdulrazak Gurnah was born in 1948 in Zanzibar and taught for many years at the University of Kent. He is the author of seven novels, including *Paradise* (shortlisted for both the Booker and the Whitbread Prizes), *By the Sea* (longlisted for the Booker Prize and awarded the RFI Temoin du monde prize), *Desertion* (shortlisted for the Commonwealth Prize) and, most recently, *Gravel Heart.*

David Herd's collections of poetry include *All Just* (Carcanet, 2012), *Outwith* (Bookthug, 2012), *Through* (Carcanet, 2016) and *Walk Song* (Equipage, 2018). He is Professor of Modern Literature at the University of Kent and a co-organiser of Refugee Tales.

J is a pharmacist who lives in the South of England with his wife and two children.

N came to the UK in 2016, was given refugee status in 2018 and is hoping to study health sciences.

Emma Parsons started a career in journalism and editing in the 1970s as a newscaster in Iran for National Iranian TV and Radio. She also co-wrote and acted in a popular Iranian TV show for children. Her awareness of policy iniquities regarding asylum seekers and refugees was first sparked when she was in Djibouti in 1979 and wrote a feature article for *The Spectator* on the conditions suffered by refugees from neighbouring Ethiopia. Her short story 'The Turf Cutters' was broadcast on BBC Radio 4 and she was the scriptwriter for *Don't Shut Me!* a drama/dance performance at Jackson's Lane Theatre, London. For the last twenty years, Emma has worked as a teacher in London schools. She has an MA in Language, Ethnicity and Education from King's College, London.

Anna Pincus is a founder and coordinator of Refugee Tales, and has worked with people in immigration detention for over ten years. She is currently Director of Gatwick Detainees Welfare Group.

R was born in Darfur and came to the UK five years ago. He currently lives in the West Midlands where he studies English and volunteers at a family centre. He has been a Refugee Tales walker for four years.

Ian Sansom is a novelist, journalist and broadcaster. His most recent book was *December Stories 1* (2018). He contributes regularly to *The Guardian* and writes and presents programmes on BBC Radio 4 and Radio 3.

Jonathan Skinner is a poet, field recordist, editor, and critic, best known for founding the journal *ecopoetics*. His poetry collections and chapbooks include *Chip Calls* (Little Red Leaves, 2014), *Birds of Tifft* (BlazeVOX, 2011), *Warblers* (Albion Books, 2010), and *Political Cactus Poems* (Palm Press, 2005). He has published numerous essays at the intersection of poetry, ecology, activism, landscape and sound studies. Skinner teaches in the Department of English and Comparative Literary Studies at the University of Warwick.

Gillian Slovo is a playwright and the author of thirteen books, including five crime novels, the courtroom drama *Red Dust*, which was made into a feature film starring Hilary Swank and Chiwetel Ejiofor, and the Orange Prize-shortlisted *Ice Road*. She co-authored the play *Guantanamo: Honour Bound to Defend Freedom*, which was staged internationally. Her research for her play *The Riots* inspired *Ten Days*. Gillian Slovo was President of English PEN from 2010 to 2013 and is a fellow of the Royal Society of Literature. She was born in South Africa and lives in London.

Lytton Smith is Associate Professor of Creative Writing and Director of the Center for Integrative Learning at SUNY Geneseo in Western Upstate New York. He has translated nine books from the Icelandic, including works by Bragi Ólafsson, Ófeigur Sigurðsson, Sigrún Pálsdóttir, Jón Gnarr, Kristín Ómarsdóttir, and Guðbergur Bergsson, as well as various poems and short stories. He is the author of the poetry collections *The All-Purpose Magical Tent* (Nightboat, 2009) and *While You Were Approaching the Spectacle But Before You Were Transformed by It* (Nightboat, 2013) as well as the chapbooks *My Radar Data Knows Its Thing* (Foundlings, 2018) and *Monster Theory* (Poetry Society of America, 2008).

Roma Tearne is a Sri Lankan born novelist and film maker living in the UK. She left Sri Lanka with her family, at the start of the civil unrest during the 1960s. She trained as a painter and filmmaker at the Ruskin School of Fine Art, Oxford and then was Leverhulme artist in residence at the Ashmolean Museum, Oxford. She has written six novels. Her fifth, *The Road To Urbino* was published by Little Brown in June 2012 to coincide with the premier of her film of that name at the National Gallery in London. She has been shortlisted for the Costa, the Kirimaya & *LA Times* book prize and longlisted for the Orange Prize in 2011 and, in 2012, the Asian Man Booker. Her sixth novel *The White City* was published in April 2017.

Jonathan Wittenberg was born in Glasgow in 1957, to a family of German Jewish origin with rabbinic ancestors on both sides. The family moved to London in 1963, where he attended University College School, specialising in classical and modern languages. He further developed his love of literature when reading English at King's College Cambridge (1976-9). He took a PGCE at Goldsmith's College, London and trained for the rabbinate at Leo Baeck College London, receiving ordination in 1987, and continued his studies to gain a further rabbinic qualification from his teacher Dr. Aryeh Strikovsky in Israel. Since then he has worked as rabbi of the New North London Synagogue. In 2008 he was appointed Senior Rabbi of Masorti Judaism in the UK.

Acknowledgements

The editors would like to thank everyone with lived experience of detention who shared their tales in this book. Thank you to the writers. Thank you to all the people involved in the planning of Refugee Tales and to those who have taken our call for an end to indefinite detention for all to parliamentarians. Thank you to our patrons Ali Smith and Abdulrazak Gurnah. Thank you to Niamh Cusack who has been a great friend to Refugee Tales. Thanks to the University of Kent. Thank you Cassie Oakman, Dorothy Sheridan, Greg Clough, Nicky Rowbottom, the PCC of St John the Apostle and Evangelist Watford, Sal Jenkinson and all the writers and actors who took part in '28 Tales for 28 Days'. Thank you to Comma Press for your support for Refugee Tales. Thank you to the Gatwick Detainees Welfare Group and everyone the GDWG has worked with in detention, whose stories inspired Refugee Tales.